The Vision of Aquinas

Darren Humby

The Vision of Aquinas

Copyright © 2006 Darren Humby

The moral right of the author has been asserted.

Apart from any fair dealing for the purposes of research or private study,
or criticism or review, as permitted under the Copyright, Designs and Patents
Act 1988, this publication may only be reproduced, stored or transmitted, in
any form or by any means, with the prior permission in writing of the
publishers, or in the case of reprographic reproduction in accordance with
the terms of licences issued by the Copyright Licensing Agency. Enquiries concerning
reproduction outside those terms should be sent to the publishers.

Matador
9 De Montfort Mews
Leicester LE1 7FW, UK
Tel: (+44) 116 255 9311 / 9312
Email: books@troubador.co.uk
Web: www.troubador.co.uk/matador

ISBN 1 905237 78 2

Cover picture © Photos.com

Typeset in 11pt Times by Troubador Publishing Ltd, Leicester, UK

Matador is an imprint of Troubador Publishing Ltd

The Vision of Aquinas is for my four angels: James, Ben and Matthew, and my guardian who gave me the strength to find the right words.

Character List

Cameron	Holds the key to the downfall of the Enlightened.
Sebastian	Cameron's father
Josh	Cameron's best friend
Emily	Sebastian's housekeeper
Mr Abigail	House master at Cameron's boarding school
Thomas Aquinas	Philosopher, interpreter of Enoch's work

The Enlightened

Malach	Cameron's guardian angel
Serapiel	Malach's consort
Michael	Leader of the Archangel Council & Commander of the Heavenly Armies
Gabriel	Archangel
Sariel	Archangel
Raquel	Archangel
Remiel	Archangel
Raphael	Archangel
Uriel	Archangel
Seir	Healer angel
Kisael	Crossing Keeper of the Sea of Souls
Zahabriel	Unicorn Cavalry Commander
Harial	Unicorn Trooper

Zephaniel	Consort to the Aleph
Asiel	Leader of the Virtues Council
Gadriel	Leader of the Principality Council
Uslael	Leader of the Dominion Council
Calliel	Leader of the Thrones Council

The Fallen

Lucifer	Prince of The Fallen
Zaebos	Grand Count of The Fallen
Samsaweel	Fallen Archangel
Jetrel	Daemon
Dalkiel	Lucifer's councillor
Dagon	Chief of the Sable Core and Fallen Cavalry
Abelech	High Commander of the Daemons
Beliel	Fallen Archangel
Busasjal	Fallen Archangel
Bernael	Captain of the Sable Core
Ertrael	Captain of the Sable Core
Beleth	Captain of the Sable Core

Prologue

The year was 1274, Thomas Aquinas looked out of the small window, blinking wearily through the shaft of light which entered. A setting summer sun helped the pathetic glow of the candles illuminate the large volumes of parchment which sat on the small, bland, wooden table. Aquinas sipped slowly from the jewelled wine goblet, his heavy eyes stung from the thin fug of candle smoke floating throughout the room. The gentle breeze caused small hypnotic smoke eddies and swirls high in the ceiling. For the past eight years he had lived in the room, his modest surroundings furnished with a small bed, a table and chair, parchment, ink and feathers. He infrequently ventured out from his self-imposed cell for some fresh air, a walk around the Italian capital to clear his thoughts. The old man particularly enjoyed the surroundings of the River Tiber, he would stand staring across the deep green waters from the middle of the Elian Bridge which led to Hadrian's mausoleum; the Castel Sant Angelo before returning to his lugubrious apartment. The bland stone bridge always afforded him spiritual inspiration. This puzzled the theologian, standing in the centre of Rome, the city built upon seven hills was bursting with religious buildings and adornments. But this particular spot for him gave the greatest inspiration and peace.

He stared wearily upon the parchments, his work was

now nearing completion. The path of his life had brought him to this very moment. Aquinas sieved through the apocryphal work of Enoch, discovered within the deserts of Africa. The code of creation seen by Enoch had now been omitted from Aquinas' reworking of the holy text. Upon completion, the parchments would be divided into four quarters and sent to the four furthest reaches of the world, Enoch's work would then be destroyed, along with it's secret.

The frail old man sat back in his chair, the wooden back rest heavily worn and as smooth as marble was now a very familiar source of support. He fidgeted with his greying wisps of hair on the side of his head, the top devoid of a single strand.

'The key will be consumed, protected by bloodline,' Aquinas' words spoke to his inner conscience softly, seeking reassurance which was not forthcoming. Pouring himself another goblet of wine, he sipped slowly allowing the wine to gently caress his lips. 'The light of faith must never be vanquished, the symbol of man's path must remain bright. The key will pass forever with the last of...'

His spoken thoughts were interrupted by a knock on the wooden door, he pulled back the heavy wrought iron lock and heaved the door open. The musty smell of the damp corridor filtered past Aquinas, pushed before the airy winds that inhabited the maze of deep corridors which fingered their way throughout the papal palaces. Aquinas watched the shadow walk along the wall of the corridor disappearing around the corner. The smell of hot broth and freshly cooked bread pulled his attention down to the floor where his servant had left his supper. His stomach grumbled in appreciation but he had no appetite and placed the tray against the opposite wall of the corridor. The philosopher's gaunt features testament to his waning health.

A stuffy chill began to set in as the heat of the day was replaced by the oppressive stickiness of the night. Aquinas once again sought the support of his chair, his work complete. In front of him sat four plain leather boxes, precise instructions were written out and attached to each. Aquinas purposefully locked each one with a small key then placed the keys into a smaller wooden box, this box was to be destroyed in the giant forge of Venazzia.

In the far corner of his room stood a highly decorated silver font, which sat atop a gold ornate cross. He carefully placed the complete original text of Enoch and the section of parchment which held the code to the creation inside the font. As he slowly shuffled back and forth from the font and the table Aquinas turned, unsettled looking at the empty far corner of the room, he shook his head annoyed with himself for being distracted by the spirits that accompanied him. His hand trembled as he brought the flickering flame of a candle closer to the wick protruding from just inside the pile of parchment; flames gradually licked across the top layer of the bundle. With a flash, flames drove deep into the pile, the sheen inside of the font began to darken.

After a wash and fresh set of clothes, Thomas Aquinas sealed the letter which expressed his wishes for the burial of his body. The wax seal displayed the coat of arms which carried the power of the papacy itself. He sighed heavily, his bones creaked in irritation as he pushed himself up from his chair. Without the support of the table Aquinas would have been hard pressed to stand independently. He shuffled over to his bed and lay on the straw filled mattress. As he allowed his weight to sink into the fabric, clouds of moon speckled dust rose skyward floating hypnotically around him. He clasped his hands together over his chest and stared up at the ceiling. A thin layer of smoke continued to hang in the room, although the smell of burnt parchment had now been replaced by the odour of rotten apples mixed with sewage wafting across the city from the River Tiber. Aquinas for the first time in many years let the release of burden flow from his body. From the courtyard below came the sound of hooves of four horses upon cobble. Their quest just beginning; his quest was complete. His eyes closed. They would never open again.

Chapter One

Present Day

Malach walked through the Gate of Arabah, gazing in awe at the huge gateway to the angel city. Set in an arch of light the Gate of Arabah was the north gate, the main thoroughfare into the city. In the far distance, upon the horizon the protector could see the seven palaces representing the universal councils. The tallest palace, a tower of pure white was flanked by the six angelic palaces; three on either side, home of the angelic councils which governed the Enlightened. Atop the taller palace of The Collective, the rays of the Aleph radiated out across the realm, a kingdom of forever light. If extinguished, perpetual darkness would prevail throughout the cosmos.

Malach strode forcefully through the streets of the city, his white cloak flapping behind him; as a protector, his wings and cloak were pure white, un-tipped by any other colour. He entered the market square which bustled with angels seeking goods to carry out their trades and duties, some sought that unusual piece of adornment for their personal wears or homes. Music and laughter filled the air, unnoticed by Malach. Maybe I am way off the mark he thought, but I need to know, I need to hear it from the council. Why Samsaweel? Why him? The protector's thoughts were filled with his earlier meeting with The Fallen archangel.

Malach had sensed a sinister air of foreboding, an uneasy feeling grew within him as the air directly in front of him pulsed gently; an unwelcome visitor emerged through the throng of people going about their business on the snow covered streets of London.

'Samsaweel I thought it was you. I am surprised it has taken so long for one of you to make an appearance.'

The archangel stepped forward, his tall, lean figure becoming clearer through the swirling snow. His black cloak hung neatly, emblazoned with the white crest of The Fallen; a dagger through the middle of two large wings.

'We are in no rush protector, time has shown the boy to be succumbing to us without any intervention' his hypnotic voice unsettled Malach.

The protector looked down at the boy peering through the large shop window. His cheeks bright red as the cold wind funnelled it's way through the chaotic business of man's world. Malach could see that Cameron had a small well of tears collecting in his eyes, unsure whether it was the usual inner pain that he had been suffering or the chilled air. He hoped it was the latter.

'The boy is not succumbing to you. He has been through a great ordeal but his faith holds firm. He will be even stronger for this experience, you are wasting your time.'

Samsaweel laughed 'Oh Malach, time is of no importance here. It is irrelevant,' he glared at Malach his black eyes piercing the falling curtain of snow. 'The outcome is the only issue.'

Malach's mind raced as he continued to march on through the lanes of the angel city. Why should I be concerned about The Fallen appearing on the scene? I knew it would have to happen the longer Cameron was locking himself away. The Fallen are opportunists who will always seek the faith of a disbeliever or any entity who shows signs of wavering - but why an archangel?

Quickening his pace Malach headed for the quay on the edge of The Sea of Souls. He turned down a narrow concourse. Small, rectangular shaped houses lined the marbled lane, vibrant colourful shades of greens, blues and reds of the window shutters stood out against the white walls. He could hear laughter and conversation waft down the corridor of houses from within. As he exited the lane, the protector could see the crossing control sitting at the entrance to the harbour, quickening his step, the urgency to speak with the council drove him on. The urge to take to the wing was only stemmed by the thought of punishment meted out to anyone other than a herald clogging the airways.

The protector fought his way through the busy harbour. Ferries emptying and loading passengers on their way to or returning from the Seven Palaces. Cargo vessels of varying sizes setting off to carry their vital wares around the kingdom. Inside the small quayside crossing control, Malach felt claustrophobic in the cramped surroundings, he coughed agitated at being kept waiting by the small, rotund clerk.

'Malach welcome, what can I do for you?' Kisael looked up at Malach over his small round glasses, then continued thumbing through endless reams of consort orders requesting an audience with the different councils. The counter was unseen through the jumble of paperwork which threatened to overwhelm the small room.

'I need to speak to the Archangel Council.'

'That should be no problem, do you know your consort order number?' Kisael stood poised ready to produce the corresponding order at the flick of a wing.

Malach placed his hands on the desk and leant forward 'I haven't got a consort order, but it is imperative I speak to the council!'

Kisael became ruffled, tutting, he removed his glasses placing them purposefully on the marbled counter.

'You know the procedure Malach. Without a consort order you cannot cross the Sea of Souls,' he said forcefully with a flamboyant wave of his hands. 'What would happen if everyone, when they liked, summoned their council?'

Kisael stood there with his head to one side looking at Malach waiting for the answer. An answer wasn't forthcoming. He replaced his glasses on the edge of his nose.

'Chaos! that is what would happen, seek your consort.'

Kisael returned to his duties. Malach knowing it was pointless to spend time arguing with him, left.

Serapiel offered Malach a chair. The cool room made the feathers on his wings tingle, he stretched them downwards, the tips of his feathers caressed the highly patterned marble floor. Onyx chimes hanging at his consort's window tinkled their song, much like the Japanese bamboo chimes the protector had seen within the entities world. He always marvelled at how both worlds carried the influences shared between them. With a deep breath Malach began to explain to his consort why he had to speak to the Archangel Council.

'The Fallen will try and undermine any entity where they can secure a weakness Malach,' said Serapiel.

Serapiel's long blonde hair complemented her purple cloak of the consorts; the tips of her wings were also purple, the sign of angelic wisdom. Consorts were the civil servants of the councils and mentors to the angels. They were usually very old angels, not in appearance but in the passing of the years and the knowledge they had gained. Every angel within the Enlightened had a consort, although not all sought their guidance, they were the only route to an audience with any of the councils or individual council members; apart from the Highest Power where only the angels of The Collective had the authority.

'It may well be just pure coincidence the darkness have sent a senior Fallen to your entity. It has happened before in the past, and I have no doubt it will happen again.'

Malach frowned. 'They have taken so long to make an appearance Serapiel. They react very quickly when an entity shows any weakness, and it is normally a daemon who makes the initial move.' He untied his cloak, placing it over the backrest of the chair, 'they are usually very subtle. The sudden appearance of a dark archangel is not exactly subtle!'

Serapiel saw the concern radiate from Malach's deep green eyes, 'your entity has shown a desire to communicate up to the point of his loss, has he not? That is very unusual in one so young, how old is he now fourteen?'

'Yes' replied Malach, 'nearly fifteen of his years.'

'Entities communicate, normally up to five of their years. Then through the teachings of their world they lose the will, never the ability, they just forget how to. In time protector you will see how far the entities have travelled down a parallel path opposite to that of the Enlightened. Whilst the majority do not actually tread along the road towards the dark, they are subjected to a barrage of teachings which denounce any suggestions that individuals can communicate through the angelic walls, as the insight of madness or childish whims.'

Serapiel paused, distracted by angels walking by her open window, their noisy chatter flooding the room. As they passed she continued.

'Few when they turn to adult years find the desire to regain the partnership they had with their protector. The majority ignore the existence of us altogether. Some go on to find the Fallen.'

Serapiel sat forward clasping her hands together. 'You will understand this once you have partnered more entities Malach. The boy is your first, it is perfectly reasonable you are concerned. In the past the boy has shown a desire to communicate, hopefully that desire will return. But be prepared, for it may not.'

Malach knew this but was unsettled by it being confirmed by his consort.

'Protector, The Fallen will seek out entities who have the will and the ability to block out human distraction to continue in the partnership of the light. If they have the ability to carry on seeking the company of their protector through the angelic wall, then why not with The Fallen? The entity may hold a longing to grow through the dark. The Fallen will test this and use any means at their disposal to achieve their aims. Any means Malach!'

Malach strolled back through the city towards the north gate. Towers either side of it dominated the immediate skyline. Imposing beacons of protection. Malach passed a cohort of The Powers on their way to take over the sentry of the city wall. Taller than most angels, The Powers were the soldiers of the Enlightened. Equipped with armour of gold, their breastplates were embossed with the image of the Aleph, the rays spreading to every part of the gleaming chest armour. Each soldier was armed with a spear and sword, the blades of pure light were the only instrument which could slay a fallen angel. Their long, white, rectangular shields, emblazoned with the gold insignia of each soldier's legion; stags, hawks and lions matched the shimmering gold of their cloaks. Powerful bows clipped to the underside of their cloaks belied their weight. The protector was always drawn to the beautiful engraved scenes from past battles with the dark which adorned each helmet, scenes flowed down the protective nose band and cheek pieces. Atop their helmets long white plumes hung majestically. Their wings were tipped with gold, colour insignia of the heavenly armies.

He felt foolish, scurrying back to the city upon the first sight of The Fallen. When he had been assigned to Cameron, he had felt a deep sense of pride and responsibility. Malach could not think of a higher calling within the Enlightened than guiding an entity through the journeys they would encounter in their life. Now he felt as if it was him who was being guided, inadequacies which were failing Cameron. Even though the angel kingdom was always covered by a state of perpetual light Malach knew it was time for evening to be returning on earth. All protectors liked to be in place when their entities slept, it was a time The Fallen looked for opportunities to seek out weaknesses. The time when man's dreams were collected, if allowed, by their protectors, or their fallen guardians, and the messages from their woken day read. Angels who accompanied entities were only able to receive the dreams and the messages within, if the entity fully believed in the reciprocal path of the Enlightened or The Fallen. The angels would battle furiously for this belief.

Malach returned to earth, more determined than ever that Cameron would receive all of his divine protection no matter what the cost.

Sebastian sat back comfortably in his chair, the log fire crackled sending a warm glow into the large Georgian dining room. He lit a large cigar, squeezing his cheeks in as he puffed, a large swirl of smoke rose above his head.

'I am going to ring Cameron's school in the morning, they may well have been badly affected by the weather. If there are any problems with the heating his new term could be delayed. Emily could you make sure Cameron's school uniform is ready.'

Emily smiled, she had been Sebastian's house keeper since Cameron was four years old. 'It's all done, everything is washed, ironed and packed in his trunk,' she replied in her soft Irish lilt.

'Thank you Emily' Sebastian said warmly. He took another puff of his cigar and leaned to one side as he looked at his son sitting at the far end of the highly polished dining table. Cameron's pale skin was almost ghostly in the shallow lighting of the dining room, the fires flickering flames caused his dancing shadow to creep across the table. The side of his head lay in his hand, a knot of black hair fell across his forehead. His shopping trip around Regents Street was an uneventful, bone-chilling wander around the shops with his father. Christmas vouchers remained safely unspent in his small leather wallet.

'You must be looking forward to seeing all your friends

again Cam?' asked his father.

Cameron's mind was occupied, he had not heard his father as he toyed with his food, his fork pushing a sprout around a maze of peas left uneaten.

'Cameron?'

'Huh' grunted Cameron sitting, staring blankly at his father.

'I said you must be looking forward to going back to school and seeing your friends, especially Josh.'

Another large swirl of smoke rose to the ceiling.

'Yes I am.' Cameron put his fork down, paused in thought before walking over to the large window, stretching awkwardly as he went.

'Are you ok?' Sebastian asked. He could see his son was once again pre-occupied. Ever since the death of Rebecca, Cameron's mother, he had become withdrawn. Sebastian found it hard to break down the barriers which had enveloped his son. The last year had been a process of building a relationship with him that had not existed when Rebecca was alive. Sebastian had grasped and begun to enjoy the newly imposed role, however unwanted through circumstance; although Cameron had thus far been unreceptive to any show of love or support.

'Just a little tired, I haven't slept very well' he pushed his hand through his hair as he stared outside, ignoring his reflection as it stared back at him.

'Have you been having the dreams again Cam?'

'Yes, but it is ok don't worry.'

Cameron peered outside, the only sign of life was the cat across the road mewing outside number forty five. Cameron tried to tidy his hair, his reflection seeming to do all it could just to make a messier knot.

'I'm going to go to my room for a while, is that ok?'

'Of course' replied his father.

As Cameron walked out of the room he turned to Emily 'Thank you for dinner, sorry I didn't eat it all.'

She smiled at him as she gathered in the plates. Sebastian looked after his son as he left the dining room and slowly made his way up the deep oak staircase. He found it difficult now to remember how things were before the death of Rebecca. The house was full of love and energy, the fervour of life permeated through every brick. His pain, his loss drove a cloak over the memories of how it was. A year; it seemed so much longer, every day without her was a lifetime.

Cameron once confident in the company of others, a mini socialite in his own right now sought the sanctuary of his own space. His dreams which troubled him so, after the accident returned. Sebastian knew they affected him far more than he let on. He wanted to understand, to help, but he knew that to press Cameron before he was ready would more than likely send his son further into the protective cocoon that he surrounded himself in.

'Hello Malach.'

The protector spun around sharply as he recognised the deep threatening voice behind him.

'Samsaweel! You have no place here,' growled Malach. A sense of consternation enveloped the protector as the realisation that the archangel's initial appearance was not merely a chance meeting.

Samsaweel looked up at the front of the Georgian terraced house, steps led up to the impressive blue door, a snow crested holly wreath still adorned it. Big windows either side of it, the lights were on inside and the curtains were not drawn. Inside, The Fallen archangel could see past the Christmas Tree to where Cameron was having supper with his father and Emily

'Oh I think at the moment it would appear I have as much right to be here as you have Malach, would you not agree?' asked Samsaweel sarcastically.

Malach knew Samsaweel was after a reaction. To provoke him would be foolish, Cameron until now had not been of any interest to The Fallen. The archangel was an opportunist, he hoped!

'I would find it very difficult to agree with you about anything' Malach replied sternly.

'The boy might agree with me' Samsaweel smirked as he gestured towards Cameron who was now standing at the window. Malach turned to see Cameron stroking his hair, attempting to flatten the rebellious strands into something resembling neatness.

'Something which The Fallen will never find out. The entity is strong, the light within him shines bright, archangel. He has no need for the path of chaos you preside over,' Malach said angrily. 'His inner strength will return in time, growing stronger as he manages to fill the gap and find his destiny. A destiny that does not include or require the company of any daemon!'

Malach purposefully stepped closer to Samsaweel, he was slightly smaller than the dark angel, and stared hard into his deep black eyes.

Samsaweel tilting his head back laughed contemptuously, 'Malach,' the dark angel took an intimidating step closer to the protector, his eyes turning even blacker as the reflection in them dimmed. 'There is no need to be so hostile!'

Samsaweel pushed aside the edge of his cloak exposing

the pearl black hilt of his sword. He patted the pommel gently with his fingers. A gesture that did not go unnoticed. The swords of The Fallen moulded in the Fires of the Damned, would cause suffering to the point where death would be the cry from the stricken. The wiry horns sprang from the edge of the hilt, entwined around each other to create a perfect guard around the handle. Samsaweel turned away, his figure slowly melted into the falling snow.

'There is no rush,' his voice carried back on the wind, 'in time the boy will show where his need lies.'

A chink of morning sunshine fought the heavy swollen clouds in the winters sky. The wind carried on it small flakes of snow which danced frantically outside Cameron's bedroom window. He stared down upon the street below, he had dreamt again last night, the images returned exactly as they did every time, turning, he looked around his room without actually seeing anything replaying the vision back to himself.

The old man scribbled frantically, the sharp edge of the feather scratched away at the parchment. A dip into the small metal pot of ink, a click as he tapped off the excess, then the words flowed again. A shaft of sunlight speared through the small open window, a corner of the top finished parchment which sat on an untidy heap lifted as a fresh breath of air rushed into the room. The old man turned the pages of a large heavy book, read for a few moments then sat back in his chair and rubbed his blood shot eyes, surrounded by dark rings caused by the sleepless nights spent in the shadowed gloom of his room. He thoughtfully glanced out of the window then returned to his scribbling.

Cameron found the dreams unsettling, mainly due to

the fact they were always about the same thing. They never changed, confused by images he had no recollection of seeing in his waking hours. He had been told dreams were complicated things, it was the brain clearing out the junk of the day, recharging itself. He shook his head, how could it be my brain is filing away things I have not seen or spoken about? he pondered. Who is the old man wearing a tabard, it looks just like the sleeveless jacket that represents my school house? The tabard has a coat of arms on it, I don't recognise it and he is writing with a feather. He then goes and lays on his bed, there's a bright light and the dream ends. Always the same, it never changes. If only I could see beyond the light he thought.

He was disturbed from his thoughts by his father, calling up the stairs.

'OK, I will be down' shouted Cameron.

He was looking forward to returning back to school. Although Josh had phoned him, what seemed like everyday, Cameron was excited about seeing his best friend again. The Christmas holiday had been long, despite his father's efforts to make the festive period as normal as possible; the absence of his mother was too big a hole to fill. He picked up his school jacket, had a long look around his room checking he had left everything where it should be. His bedroom seemed a lot larger with everything tidied away, order was always instilled into him by his father, his mother used to have a more laissez faire attitude to his lived in environment.

Cameron walked over to his bed and picked up the photograph sitting on the shelf above it. A folded piece of paper fell to the floor. Forgetting the letter was propped behind the picture frame; he carefully opened the letter, and began to read. He looked over towards the cupboard in the corner of his room, hidden inside lay a forgotten parcel;

>Dear mum,
>
>Emily told me it would help if when I needed to I wrote to you. She said you would be able to read it, I hope she is right. I miss you very much. I try not to cry, it is very hard, but I think you would be very proud of me. I never let anyone see my tears, I wait until I am alone or find somewhere people cannot see me. I don't understand why you had to die. Dad says it is because God needed you in heaven more than we do, I can't say that he is right. I think he says it because it makes him feel better. I am trying to look after him, you would be pleased we now spend as much time together as we can. He has tried to cut back on his work when I am home from school. I haven't been to see you since, I can't face it but I hope you have seen the flowers Emily has brought you from me, but I did write the card. I have lot's to tell you about mum, I will write again but I had better go to sleep or dad will notice the light on. I brought you a Christmas present. I have wrapped it and hidden it, so you don't find it.
>
>I miss you very much mum, merry xmas
>Cam XX

Cameron folded the letter, wiped away a tear and stared into the warm brown eyes, rubbing her cheek with his finger. He was never free of the memories of his mother, even during busy moments she would drift to the back of his mind but was always there. As soon as his mind was free of thought his mother would return straight to the front of his senses. Her face, voice, even her smell would drift throughout him. The smile which came back at him made him return a soft smile, but his heart was heavy.

Emily fussed and flapped, it was the only time Cameron ever noticed her let down her calm manner. He could smell the scent of freshly cooked bread on her apron, as she handed him a Tupperware box full of small parcel pastries, their contents a surprise until bitten into. Emily always hated when he returned to school, the house lost it's meaning, Sebastian spent long periods away from it's warmth and since Rebecca's death she had found it increasingly more difficult.

'Bye for now Cam, now make sure you write to your father every week' Emily helped him put his jacket on. 'Everything is packed away in your trunk.'

'Thank you Emily' replied Cameron warmly. He tucked the Tupperware box under his arm and followed his father down to the waiting car.

Cameron was very fond of Emily. She always had the ability to know what to say, when to say it and when to do something just before it was needed, but more importantly in Cameron's opinion when just to leave well alone, her timing impeccable.

'Morning sir' the chauffer bowed his head, his cap held under his arm.

'Morning, where is Bradshaw?' asked Sebastian quizzically.

'Called in sick sir. So they allocated me over to you this morning' the driver replied opening the car door.

'Your name?' asked Cameron's father. Sebastian looked the chauffer up and down finding some reassurance in his immaculate appearance.

'Thompson sir.' The chauffeur brushed his jacket down as a few rogue snowflakes found their way onto the plush fabric.

Sebastian knelt and held his son by the tops of his arms. 'Cam I will ring you later, if not this evening, tomorrow. I would like you to come home this weekend. I know it is your first week at school but next week I go away and would like to see you before I go.'

'Ok' said Cameron.

Sebastian pulled Cameron closer, kissing him on the side of his head as he held him. Cameron pulled away embarrassed by the outward show of emotion in front of the whole world. The snow crunched under his feet as he walked over to the open car door, before getting in, he turned seeing his father staring back at him. Cameron smiled warmly, then jumped in before his father had time to smile back.

The long monotonous drive was broken as the car left the motorway. In the distance heavy clouds sat low on the pale hills, Cameron looked up at the threatening sky ready to lay even more snow on the white blanket covering the fields and towns. He noted it was a slightly brighter day even though the sun struggled to break through.

Cameron felt hungry; it was a long time since breakfast and with a expectant sense of surprise he lifted the lid off the Tupperware box, entwined smells of meat, onions, fruits and pastry filled the car. His stomach growled appreciatively.

'Have you had a good Christmas sir?' asked Thompson.

Cameron looked up, he had not spoken a word since the start of the journey and was quite expecting to have a silent trip all the way to Byford. Like his father Cameron noted the chauffeur was very well presented, even when he had removed his cap Cameron noted not a single strand of hair was out of place. He had an unusual aroma about him, it was not an aftershave that Cameron had ever smelt before. The only thing remotely similar was the scent of cinnamon Emily used frequently in her cooking.

'Yes thank you' replied Cameron politely, as he continued to look out of the window. He popped two small pastry parcels in his mouth, the taste of meat and onion of one in stark contrast to sweet apple of the other.

'Did you get everything you wished for? You know for Christmas.'

Cameron did not reply straight away, he continued to finish his mouthful.

'Not everything.'

He squinted into the distance as the light from the icy landscape reflected back at him.

Thompson quickly glanced at him, Cameron was not a small boy for his age but he thought how pitiful his demeanour looked as he sat in the chair next to him. His frame was carried with a heavy burden, a saddle which stifled the confidence and swagger present a long time ago.

'Maybe Santa will bring it for you next year.' He said flippantly.

Cameron glared up at Thompson, frowning.

'There is no such thing as Father Christmas! Even if there was it wouldn't matter whether I have been good or bad, or what I think or do.' He lowered his voice 'even if he was real, he could never bring me what I really want.'

Thompson continued to look straight ahead, the winding rural roads had not received the same treatment from the gritting lorries as the major trunk roads. A thin layer of snow covered the icy road urging an unwary driver to loose control and slide into the hedgerows; Thompson appeared unconcerned to the dangers.

'It matters not about the real or unreal presence of Santa Claus, but it matters a great deal whether you have been good or bad' said Thompson.

'Why?' snapped Cameron, popping another small pastry parcel into his mouth.

'It shapes the man you become, the impact you have on the world and the ones you love.' Thompson saw Cameron was listening. 'I reckon more importantly, it is the impact on the people you don't love which is the most precious thing.'

'Why does it matter, if you are a good person, bad things happen. My mum…' Cameron held his breath, he had rarely spoken of his mother to the three most important people in his life, let alone a complete stranger. Sebastian would have dealt with the subject deftly, but thus far had been relieved his son had largely avoided the subject. Emily waited patiently, never pressing the subject knowing Cameron would talk about his loss when he felt it necessary. Josh did not care, in the boyish manor of there was always something far more important than dealing with emotion of any sort. Cameron continued forcefully 'my mum was a good person!'

Thompson took his eyes off of the road, he looked at Cameron seeing the grey aura which surrounded him.

'Your mum was a wonderful person, who loved you,

who loves you very much.'

Cameron turned away. He recognised the fields and the wood in the distance. He thought the snow covered trees resembled a scene from a magical film; dragons, wizards and dwarves all living and vying for superiority of The Great Wood! An untouched world of fantasy. The car entered the school gates, drove up the long, winding drive towards the school halls.

'Thank you Thompson' said Cameron as he stepped out of the car.

Thompson closed the car door. 'You are very welcome. Remember Cameron the strength of a man is how he deals with adversity. It is no different even in your young years, you will find your path, depend on the people you trust, open yourself to their warmth and spirit.'

Cameron did not reply, Malach watched as his entity climbed the steps, he was glad he had communicated with Cameron, he hoped his words had made a small difference. There was far more he would have liked to have said, but for now it was enough. Cameron reached the door of the school, the words echoing in his head, he turned to say thank you once again but Thompson and the car had already gone. Looking across the school grounds, he had not heard the car drive away and wondered how it could have disappeared so quickly as small flakes of snow began to turn into larger heavier flakes. He bent down to pick up his trunk, as he did so, a large white feather landed on top of the brown lid. He picked it up, twiddling it in his fingers as he looked up into a bird less sky.

At the far end of the pantheon Zaebos sat on the Throne of Azazel. The throne belied the sombre air of the great hall; a chair of iridescent blue light swirled with differing shades from the bottom to the very tips of the backrest's carved wings which rose into the air. A tall heavy set angel, the Grand Count of The Fallen answered only to Lucifer himself, his ruthlessness across all the kingdoms legendary. Flickering orbs set in iron beckets on the walls gave life to the shadows dancing around the cavernous room.

'So his protector, will it be difficult to get to the boy?'

'He is of no concern to me Zaebos' Samsaweel replied stepping forward towards the dais. The huge throne was flanked on either side by the dark angel soldiers of the Sable Core, legions of The Fallen, 'when the time comes the protector will be dealt with.'

Zaebos stood and grabbed at the corner of the robe of wolf pelt which hung over his broad shoulders. He rubbed his chin, Samsaweel noted the waves of thought forming deep lines across his forehead. The grand count stepped down from the dais slowly and approached Samsaweel, menacingly lowering his voice.

'No concern? If we alert the Enlightened, all will be lost. There must be nothing out of the ordinary to rouse their suspicions.' He paused 'am I understood archangel?' Zaebos clenched his fist, 'we know the visions have once again returned to the boy, as I knew they would. What we do not know is how far he can see into the dream. The images will become stronger and will ultimately lead us to the key of Enoch. Once we have the key, the Enlightened will have no defence. Lucifer will rule, the kingdoms will become one.'

He returned to the throne, 'I think it would be good if the boy is approached by his kind, to continue to work on his misgivings.'

'Is that wise my lord,' interjected Samsaweel. 'I mean to say that any hint the boy receives about his dreams may well alert him to our cause. Would it not be better to allow only the daemons to accompany him?'

'The daemons will make sure he knows what to do. But any weakness we can use to forward our cause must be exploited. It may only be a small gesture but added together these will bring a greater doubt upon the boy. Samsaweel I want you to keep a very close eye on everything. But keep your distance. Whilst it is imperative we gain the confidence of the entity, it is vital the Enlightened are not made suspicious by the presence of anyone higher than a daemon.'

Samsaweel bowed, turned and walked towards the great doors, the image of Azazel carved on one, Semhaza on the other. Two of the original fallen angels who joined Lucifer turning against the path of the Aleph. They were now imprisoned in the Void of Damnation for all eternity, captured by Michael and the heavenly armies. The archangel walked past the great pillars rising high towards the vaulted ceilings, each one covered in emblems of the dark world. The daemons were the lowest level of angel in the hierarchy of The Fallen. Mischief makers and messengers of ruin, they sought the weaknesses in man's faith, chinks in the armour of belief, when an entity showed a desire, however small the daemons attempted to sow the seeds of doubt and darkness. They were the vanguard of The Fallen's objective in turning man away from the protective wings of the angel kingdom; merciless whenever the opportunity presented itself, they would revel in the slaying of a protector.

Cameron lay on his bed in the dormitory, taking the opportunity of the quiet whilst the other boys spent the break between classes playing football outside, studying in the library or generally milling about. His art project he had been working on during the holiday was nearly finished. He had used it as a convenient distraction whilst at home to spend long spells in his bedroom. Even during the day, the dark oak flooring and fascia of the dormitory held a murky gloominess, requiring the small wall lights to be on all the time.

'Hello Cameron.'

Cameron looked up to see his art teacher and house leader standing by his bed. Despite his cautious dislike of Mr Abigail he politely said hello. He had never been able to put a finger on why he had not warmed to him. Apart from sports, art was his favourite lesson, and Mr Abigail was an excellent tutor. Cameron put it down to the fact that he could not possibly like everyone, there were boys in the school that, whilst he did not hate, he kept a comfortable distance from.

'How are you? I see you are working on your project. May I?' Mr Abigail held out his hand, Cameron closed the graphics folder and handed it to him.

The teacher flicked through the pages, stopping at points of interest.

'As usual it would appear to be a fine piece of work. What is the text about behind the artwork?'

'The project is about heaven sir'

'Interesting,' replied Mr Abigail 'and what do you know about heaven?'

Cameron paused for a moment. 'It is where people go when they die. I am told it is the kingdom of God and his angels, that's where they look over us, protecting everyone on earth.'

Cameron took back his work and flicked through the pages he had been working on.

'It would appear your project has a greater depth than just mere artwork. You could ask yourself whether the artwork represents what you believe or what you question. Does God and his angels look after everyone?'

The art teacher walked between the beds in the dormitory, disappearing into shadow then light as he passed the inadequate wall lights, hands clasped behind his back in his usual manner. The habits of a life in teaching were hard to forget.

'Do you think angels look after everyone down here?'

Cameron thought hard before answering, he grew angry. Surely anyone who knew what he had been through would not have needed to ask such a question. Before he could answer Mr Abigail continued.

'Unfortunately you have discovered recently they watch over only those who serve their purpose.'

'I don't understand why she died' Cameron remarked swallowing the lump in his throat, he had started to learn how to be stronger inside and not allow the tears to fall.

'Well there are some who would say the image of heaven is not how we would like it to be, or are taught.' Mr Abigail moved closer knowing he had Cameron's attention. 'Heaven is a place where man is expected to live in servitude, a slave of the so called angels. They do their bidding on people who are led to believe they will receive ever lasting life, but the reality is far from that.'

'How do you mean?' asked Cameron softly.

'Well, let's look at your loss Cameron, as you say you

don't understand why your mum had to die? What purpose was there in her leaving you so suddenly. I bet before it all happened you believed in angels and heaven didn't you?'

'Yes I did.'

'What did they do to repay you for your belief? They took your mum, is that how heaven and the angels look after us? We believe in them, attend church, you have to attend Sunday church when you are resident at the weekends. How has it benefited you?'

Cameron did not respond as Mr Abigail turned and left the dormitory. His work done.

Although confused by the conversation the words had a resonance. Cameron looked around him, sensing an unexplained pressure; a pulse. He recognised the feeling when he was in the car with Thompson, and a few times before his mother died. He was certain he caught a gentle waft of cinnamon, before he could confirm it, it was gone.

Malach was disturbed. He knew the words spoken by Mr Abigail were not directed at Cameron in a healthy theological way. His words were manipulative. Pacing around Cameron's bed space he wondered whose purpose Abigail's conversation had served. Malach began to sense the familiar air of foreboding which represented the presence of The Fallen; although not as strong as when Samsaweel had first appeared, it grew in intensity. The dormitory dimly lit added to the air of dread, it was an old Victorian building with high ceilings. The small wall lights evenly spaced around it's perimeter cast a dim glow. Each pupil's bedside cabinet had a lamp, only Cameron's was on. The protector's senses were now alert, he felt the presence of The Fallen but could not see them. This was a very dangerous time. He stood perfectly still, pushed aside the right hand side of his cloak, with a swirl it robed over his left shoulder. Placing the palm of his right hand on the top of his sword's pommel, Malach began to take one cautious step at a time, moving around the beds of the dormitory, his movements were an unconscious action, every step deliberate. Malach was using the ominous pulse of The Fallen to guide him. He glanced from side to side purposefully seeking to pierce the gloom. The presence grew stronger, his hand coiled tightly around his sword's hilt.

He caught the subtle shift of air and moved his shoulder within a split second of the dark blade falling. It missed and carried on it's downward journey, a journey that expected to slice him in two, sending him into the hands of damnation. Malach swiftly drew his sword from it's scabbard and with a flick of his wrist he parried the daemon's next attack. The daemon, fast and experienced, glided around the room his attacks swift and silent. The murkiness giving his movements some protection.

The protector felt the strength of his attacker as he blocked an attack lifting his sword over his head, his blade stopping just short of his scalp. With all his strength he pushed the daemon away, bringing his sword down to strike at the daemon's hip. With a deft sidestep his blade was swept to one side, only by strengthening his grip on the handle did he manage to stop his blade flying across the dormitory. The force of the blow sent him spinning sideways. The daemon lunged. His blade struck Malach's unprotected forearm, slicing downwards cutting deep into his arm.

Malach yelled, the pain surged deep into his body

forcing him to his knees. His immediate world blurred, his consciousness began to ebb away as the pain drove deeper.

The daemon unclipped his cloak and stepped forward confidently as it fell to the ground. Malach sensing the end, tried to stand up, pain drove ever deeper into his body causing him to double over again. Desperate, his thoughts were a blur of death, paralysis and survival. Mockingly the daemon stood victorious over his vanquished prey, he lifted his sword with both hands, readied himself to drive the blade in between Malach's shoulders, he thrust downwards.

A flash of light swirled. The daemon's chest took the full impact of Malach's blade, sinking deep into his chest. The dark angel faltered, taking small unsteady steps backwards, grasping at the sword but the fatal blow was dealt. The blade was pure light the only thing which could bring down one of The Fallen. He slumped to his knees then fell sideways.

Pain forced it's way throughout Malach's body, the protector grimaced, enveloped in a burning grip of torment. Malach felt as if he was being lowered into the Fires of the Damned, his vision blurred then fell dark.

Whilst it was not unusual for The Fallen to attempt to take the life of a protector, the attempt tallied with the appearance of the high ranking fallen angel, Samsaweel, demanded the attention of the Archangel Council.

Michael represented the majestic power and faith that was the Enlightened. He was the head of the Archangel Council and the Commander in Chief of the Heavenly Armies, his throne was elevated higher than his six fellow members of the Archangel Council. To the left of him sat

Raguel, Sariel and Remiel. To his right sat Gabriel, Raphael and Uriel. He stared down at the summoned consort.

Serapiel stood in front of the dais, the seven council members sat quietly as she explained the conversation she recently had with Malach. Behind them the continuous gentle rumble of water filled the hall, the Falls of the Divine started from nowhere, emerging from thin air at the far end of the chamber behind the dais; it continued downwards and fell far below into the Sea of Souls. The gentle noise in stark contrast to their size, a majestic symbol of angelic power. Chased cherubs decorated the ceiling, dancing down the four pillars that towered in the four corners of the hall.

Michael stood, tugging at his lapis blue cloak, his wings were tipped with the gold of the heavenly armies and the lapis blue of the archangels.

'We have recovered Malach. He will live. He has been extremely fortunate, The Fallen have taken the light from twenty three protectors since the last moon. This attack on the protector in itself is not an incident which warrants concern, but I have heard of the interest of the fallen archangel.'

'Has it not always been the way of The Fallen to seek out weaknesses in any entity?' asked Raquel fervently. 'Man has always been the focus of their strategy to bring us to our knees and spread darkness throughout our kingdom and theirs. Why would this entity merit the attention of Samsaweel?'

'I cannot explain why sire,' replied Serapiel, 'although I believe the boy is very special, I do not think Malach truly realises how so. Before his mother passed through The Gates of Righteousness, the boy was actively in communication with his protector. He has shown an ability to block, for want of a word, the teachings and prejudices that grow within man's kingdom. The boy I suspect has a greater ability.' Serapiel took breath, the council members did not interrupt, 'he may well be able to see his protector. Something not known for many moons. This is Malach's first, it is unfortunate because the entity may well be too strong for him.'

Serapiel left the council chamber, her reasons for the appearance of Samsaweel seeking the possible weaknesses within the boy were plausible. Michael stepped down from the dais and crossed the chamber floor. Serapiel was a very respected and knowledgeable consort, her opinions would not be lightly dismissed.

'We should heed her thoughts, the entity would be very useful to The Fallen, hence the appearance of Samsaweel,' Remiel said, 'we cannot just allow her words to be left, the boy's scrolls need to be viewed.'

'For what purpose? The scrolls cannot be changed we all know that' replied Michael.

Michael looked out of the arched window. In the far distance he could just make out the two towers of the Gates of Arabah, beyond them he could see the two snow tipped mountain peaks that separated the angel kingdom from the realm they served; and more importantly from The Fallen.

'What is written can never be altered even by the highest power.' Michael returned to the dais and took his seat in the centre of the arc. He turned to look at the solemn faces of the other six archangels. 'Every event has consequences which are far reaching, to change one would affect an infinite amount of scrolls already written, and those which are as yet unwritten. No it is impossible.'

'Can we not change the protector?' asked Sariel.

'No, the protector is allocated at the time the scroll is written' said Gabriel turning to his fellow council members, 'the Dominions would never allow it. Since the creation of man the scroll is the highest possible law, if we changed every protector who did not seem to be communicating and assisting their entity to our liking, then the balance would not exist and neither would we. The boy, whilst his protector remains in the care of the healers is on his own. Once the protector has healed they will both have to journey along the same paths, we will soon see what the scrolls hold for them.'

Chapter Two

Cameron's first week back at school kept him very busy, catching up with all the holiday gossip with his friends, the new school timetable and term projects to complete. New school houses had also been allocated. Cameron's new house was Nelson, this was great news. The Napoleonic wars, especially naval history, was his biggest interest. His best friend Josh was also in the same school house which Cameron found very reassuring. They had been friends from the very first day, their bed space had been next to each other since the very first night, they shared from that moment on their fears and anxieties, hopes and dreams.

Cameron was slightly larger than most of the boys in his year; he enjoyed playing rugby, cricket and football, and excelled in fencing. He found his studies a chore, something he held in common with Josh, and most of the boys at Byford for that matter. A popular boy, his calm demeanour and sense of humour found many friends in the tough public school environment.

Just before the turn of the 20th century, Byford Boy's School had once been a large Victorian estate which sat in acres of rural countryside. The long drive led up to the house from the school gates, either side grassy fields during the summer would be the playing fields, cricket field, football and rugby pitches. To the back of the school a winding path led down to Crawford Lake, named after the first headmaster. This vast expanse of water now glossed over with ice would be the venue for the school's rowing regatta in the summer months. Upon the edge of the lake sat the overgrown wood, seen by Cameron on his way into the school. It stretched for miles, the vast majority of it not seen by human eyes for many years. Stories of haunting and goblins were passed down through the generations of boys. Only the bravest dared to venture past the tree line.

Josh had been a constant source of strength for Cameron over the past year. He was able to do things with him which did not involve 'how are you feeling?' or 'do you miss your mum?' or 'your mum now sits with the angels and watches over you.' Whilst Josh knew, he did not care much, the event was far too difficult for him to comprehend or particularly want to. His pet rabbit dying was the nearest thing to Cameron's loss that he could think of, ashamedly this was a relief, always being moaned at for not feeding it or cleaning the bedding.

'What do you think of Mr Abigail Josh?' asked Cameron, his breath misting as they slid with each footstep down the winding pathway.

'Oh he is ok, a bit odd but ok' replied Josh.

They continued tentatively towards Crawford Lake. It was early morning, a free session, so Cameron and Josh thought they would go and get some fresh air before maths. The morning was bitter, crisp air surged into their lungs as they breathed in. Tears ran down their cheeks as the soft breeze blew across the open landscape.

'Why?' asked Josh.

'Just wondered. He said some things when he was looking at my art project a few days ago.'

'What did he say about it? I thought it was brilliant,

better than mine I have a feeling you spent longer on yours than I did. I mean you were doing it every time I rang over the holidays,' jibed Josh as he released a small but rock hard snow ball at Cameron's head. The snow ball missed by a whisker.

'He didn't say anything about the work, I think he liked it, it was just…..' Cameron paused.

'What?'

'Well, he said some things about heaven and he mentioned mum, that's all, just been on my mind a little bit.'

Cameron gathered up some snow, his hands and fingers flushed red as he packed it together. His throw was inch perfect, honed skills on the cricket field.

'Whoa, you nearly had my eye out!' shouted Josh.

Cameron laughed softly under his breath, 'that's ok, the snowball could have replaced it. Plenty of time before the summer thaw to find a decent glass marble.'

Josh readjusted his hat, it was at least two sizes too big and the blue and white bobble hung awkwardly down the side of his head, swinging wildly as he walked.

'I know I don't mention it much Cam, you know, and you can tell me to shut up, but what did Abigail say about your mum then?'

Cameron thought how best to explain it to Josh, he did not think that his best friend would identify with the senses that he had about many of the things that revolved around 'the other side'.

'I think he was saying heaven may be not the kind of place we think it is. That people die whether they are good or bad?'

'But we know that anyway.' Josh interrupted.

'No I didn't mean it like that. There is no difference in heaven, no distinction between good or bad. If you believe in God, he doesn't actually care whether you do or don't. I think he meant we are the slaves of the angels, like their toys and they do as they will.' Cameron took another pause, breathing deeply, the fresh cold morning air burned his airways. 'Did that make sense?'

'Sort of,' said Josh.

'Do you believe in God Josh?' Cameron paused. 'Do you believe in angels?'

'Yes I think I do. I know my parents do.'

'I know my dad does, he said mum was taken by the angels. That she was meant to look over us both and because she was such a beautiful person, he said God needed her in heaven to help him, look over him and me. If I spoke to her even though I can't see her, she can see and hear me,' Cameron said reflectively.

'Well I've heard my dad say something like that about nanny Wilkes, so I guess they both can't be wrong can they?'

'Suppose' replied Cameron.

The boys continued on their slippery journey down towards the knoll by the lake. Josh very quickly forgot about the conversation, Cameron wouldn't.

Samsaweel headed towards the great hall. Summoned to a council of The Fallen hierarchy he knew there would be trouble. The daemon had made a very grave mistake in attacking Malach. His life did not concern The Fallen, but the angel kingdom becoming aware of their plans would. At least he would not lose his life at the hands of Zaebos which would have been infinitely worse than being slain by the protector Samsaweel thought.

The long corridor flickered with the light of becketed blue orbs. As The Fallen archangel approached the hall, a row of guards from the Sable Core stood either side of the corridor like statues. Their black chest armour reflected the dancing light of the orbs. Their tall pointed oval shields, black as coal with the white dagger and wings crest standing out in sharp contrast. Their helmets, black with long white plumes running from the top of the helmet down the back gave the impression they were taller than they actually were. Their sable eyes were bright through the cheek pieces. Powerful wings tipped with black sat through their black cloaks. Each held a thick spear, and carried heavy swords at the hip.

As Samsaweel approached the great doors of the hall, they began to open. A wall of noise struck him as he entered into the great chamber, then silence. He baulked at the sudden quietness but continued on towards the great throne. Within the crowd of angels summoned, he recognised fellow archangels, Beliel and Busasjal sitting on serpent chairs to the left of him as he walked towards the dais, the pearl black carved heads of the snakes twisted as one glaring at Samsaweel as he walked past, their forked tongues seeking his scent. Abelech, High Commander of the Daemons and Bernael, Ertrael and Beleth, Captains of the Sable Core, sat on his right. Smoke from two large open fires, one on either side of the hall, churned high in the ceiling, the gloom became thicker towards the edges of the cavernous room casting deep shadows. Samsaweel approached the dais, on either side of the steps leading up to the Throne of Azazel stood guards of the Sable Core. Upon the throne sat Lucifer. He knelt down on one knee and bent forward, paying homage to the Prince of The Fallen.

'Samsaweel' the deep stabbing voice ran through him, he tightened, and stayed low in a sign of loyal servitude, 'I have heard good things about you.'

Samsaweel cautiously lifted his head. Lucifer sat confidently on his throne, leaning to one side with his chin resting in his fingers. He was an awesome angel. Black eyes pierced the darkness. His black wings twitched powerfully, disturbing the swathes of smoke lingering above his throne. Lucifer stood, towering above any other angel in the room, he stepped forward the air pulsed away from him.

'Recent events however,' Lucifer pointed his staff at Samsaweel, the hall now silent apart from the crackle of the fires. 'Have been far from satisfactory.'

The archangel stayed down on bended knee, a mixture of pure dread and anger filled his whole being. He was about to take the full wrath of Lucifer for the stupidity of a daemon. An overwhelming urge to shout out built up within him, but he suppressed it, knowing it would be extremely foolish to interrupt.

'Zaebos informs me he made it quite clear caution was ordered, the suspicions of the Enlightened' the words hissed from his mouth, 'were not to be roused.'

Samsaweel noticed the Grand Count standing next to the throne move nervously as Lucifer mentioned his name. Even Zaebos knew the wrath of the dark prince was not something to be taken lightly.

Samsaweel thought very carefully about his reply before answering. The next few words could well be his last.

'My prince, the daemon faltered, luckily for him he was slain by the protector. He would not have stood in front of you and deserved your benevolence.'

Lucifer roared, his laughter sending a chill throughout all those present. Samsaweel closed his eyes hoping for a quick end.

'Be careful Samsaweel, for your benevolence will lead you into the Fires of the Damned!' the words drove deep into the archangel.

'My Lord!' the voice came from the corner of the hall within the shadows behind the throne. Dalkiel, Lucifer's councillor stepped into the gloomy light. He served only Lucifer, no one else. A small, ferrety angel. His shifty eyes saw everything that went on within The Fallen, Dalkiel made sure his master was informed. The councillor, or informant to the vast occupants of The Fallen city, was disliked intensely, it was only the fear of Lucifer's ire which kept him from feeling the stab of an assassin's blade. Only Dalkiel would have the impertinence to speak without being summoned to.

'Our caution and anxiety may be blinding us to the effects that our actions have.'

Lucifer returned to his throne. Dalkiel bowed and approached. The muffled words of discontent rose around the hall as he turned towards the assembled leaders of The Fallen. He confidently paced up and down the hall.

'Caution could be our downfall' he said fervently 'to change our approach would bring disaster to our cause. The Enlightened would surely question any opportunity not taken. If they suspect anything our plans would be in danger. My Lord, we need time to bring the boy to us willingly, it is the only way we will, can, succeed.'

The hall remained silent. Then a few started to whisper amongst themselves.

'Dagon, what do you think?' asked Lucifer.

Dagon stood and stepped into the middle of the hall, the Chief of the Sable Core and The Fallen Armies, a powerful, heavy set angel, possessed a quick, calculating mind. He was an experienced warlord, respected amongst all of the hierarchy.

'Dalkiel has a point, my prince' it was difficult for Dagon to admit the councillor may have been right, but he always spoke his mind no matter what and to who. 'The Enlightened are always on their guard knowing we will always strike at them given the chance, they would suspect something if we backed off.' Dagon turned to look at the faces of the assembled group, his black cloak gliding behind him. 'Maybe the distraction lies elsewhere.'

'Go on!' Lucifer ordered.

'We attack!'

The hall stirred with excitement.

'What do you mean Dagon?' asked Dalkiel under his breath, cautiously stepping nearer to the massive frame of the commander, his eyes squinting quizzically as he stared at him.

'A distraction, concentrating their focus away from the entity. We increase the targeting of all protectors. We send legions to their realm. We mass under the two peaks threatening to attack the kingdom. The boy would fade very quickly from their thoughts.'

The room exploded in noise, spear shafts stamped on the floor in approval. Raucous calls for the attack upon the angel kingdom to start straight away echoed around the cavernous chamber.

Lucifer stood, the room instantly fell silent.

'We will attack, but let the battle now commence with a

strike at man's faith. We will strike at his nations. Let us draw the Enlightened into the jaws of the dark, attack the messengers of their false prophet, spread chaos and misinformation. We will draw their minds away from the key to their downfall. We will mass under the two peaks. Terror will spread throughout the kingdom of light as they witness the power of The Fallen. The entity will, as you say, very quickly fade from their priorities!'

Cameron arrived home on Friday evening, his first week at school presented him with many new issues which started to mull away in his mind. He found it increasingly difficult to shut away all the questions he had. All continued to remain unanswered. Mr Abigail's interest in his project, or rather the art teacher's interest in Cameron's thoughts about angels, had not diminished throughout the week since the conversation in his dormitory. Any opportunity he got he would show a will to question and debate the topic of heavens worth, Cameron had begun to understand the arguments against the beliefs he held before his mother died. Why was it so different to what I have been taught and told, he questioned. Surely this is because these people have never been through the hurt I have, how could they?

Josh had been a valuable aid in mulling over all the thoughts Cameron grappled with. His best friend had a very black and white attitude to almost everything, and once again had brought an air of common sense to the conversations. He would miss him this weekend and promised he would ring him.

During the journey home he questioned Bradshaw about Thompson. The stand in driver had also been on his mind all week, it was just another confusing feeling he could not shift from his mind. Over the years Cameron had been driven to destinations by many different drivers, none had affected him as Thompson had, especially through such a short seemingly innocuous meeting. The conversation, no, thought Cameron, the feelings that clouded the journey. He struggled to find a reason for the strangely familiar presence he had about Thompson. Bradshaw had never heard of a driver called Thompson. He thought it may have been possible he was brought in through an employment agency; but he had only phoned in sick with awful stomach cramps an hour before he should have started work, so thought it unlikely. Cameron was unsurprised, he almost expected Bradshaw to say that.

When Cameron had left for school the Christmas decorations had still been in place, now taken down he thought the house looked very bland and strangely larger. After his bath he headed for the source of the smell which wafted throughout the house. The kitchen was warm and welcoming.

'Hello Cameron, feel better for your bath?' Emily said greeting him with a broad smile. Her hair was up in a messy bun, loose strands fell down the side of her face, shallowing her pretty round features.

'Yes thanks Emily. Something smells really good what is it?' asked Cameron.

'Rabbit casserole' replied Emily, lifting the casserole pot out of the oven. She placed the pot on the side and lifted the lid, swirls of steam rose joyously skywards.

Cameron stirred the casserole with a wooden spoon, wisps of hot steam floated away gently disappearing into the air, when he finished he placed his hand in the oversized oven glove and replaced the lid.

'Do you know what time father will be home?'

'When he left this morning he said he hoped to be home about seven, any later and he was going to ring,' Emily checked the time on her wrist watch which was coated in flour. 'It's almost six o'clock now so I would have thought that if he was going to be any later we would have heard.'

She continued to skilfully roll a pin, flattening with precision the pastry cover for the fruit pie.

'Emily….' said Cameron with a thoughtful pause.

'Yes.'

'Why did mum die?' Cameron did not look up at Emily, he stayed focused on the ever stretching piece of pastry.

The question startled her but she outwardly stayed very calm, Cameron had rarely spoken of the accident or his mother. She had stayed aloof from the grief which had filled the house, she grieved privately of course. But thought when Cameron was ready, when the time was right, he would open up.

'It was her time Cam. Our path is mapped out well before we are born. We all have a destiny to fulfil. For some this is grand achievements, for others it is a more sedate existence. But, we all have a role to play.' Emily placed the pastry cover over the fruit pie, offering Cameron the knife so he could trim the edges. 'Your mother was a beautiful, gentle person. She brought you into this world. But, it was her time to leave us.'

Cameron very slowly trimmed the pastry, slicing effortlessly through the wafer thin pastry, which fell into a neat pile on the counter.

'Do you believe in heaven, I mean really believe in heaven?' Cameron asked passionately.

Emily was a religious person and faith was very

important to her. Cameron knew this and thought she of all the adults he knew would have an opinion he valued. He would have asked his father but thought he would receive a more unbiased stand point to his questions from Emily.

'Of course I do!' Emily's soft Irish accent grew harder. 'Belief is all things to all men. You will find some people do not believe at all. They.....' she paused as she thought about her inner most feelings, her voice returning to a warmer softer lilt. 'They believe when you die that is it, nothing else. Some believe when you die the angels carry you to God's mansion.' She picked up the neatly trimmed fruit pie and twirled it deftly in her hands 'That is beautiful Cam, let's pop it into the oven.' Emily opened the oven, the air quivered as the heat blasted into the kitchen. 'It takes an opened mind to accept the idea. When someone has been hurt as you have been then it becomes very difficult to see any positives or reasons. It takes a strong young man to see beyond all the bad things in the world.'

'So how did you feel when you lost someone?' he asked. The neat pile of pastry trimmings were now deftly rolled into a perfect ball. Cameron rolled it round and round with the palm of his hand.

Emily stared out of the kitchen window, misted over as the cold exterior sucked the heat from the room within. She played with the dishes in the sink without achieving any kind of worthwhile cleaning.

'A great sense of loss, it is only natural that you would. I have only two sisters and one brother still alive. It doesn't get any easier to deal with Cam. It is just the understanding of it that becomes clearer.'

'Sometimes I feel her' Cameron said.

Emily dried her hands, walked over to him and put her

arm around his shoulders giving him a gentle squeeze.

'Your mother is always with you Cameron.'

'Sometimes I think I feel other things too' Cameron said softly half hoping Emily had not heard him. He took a bottle of juice from the fridge and poured himself a glass, then sat back down at the table.

'What sort of things?' Emily stopped washing up again, dried her hands once more and sat down at the kitchen table opposite Cameron.

'Well…..' Cameron had never mentioned it to anybody, not even Josh. But he knew Emily would listen to him and not make him feel silly. 'I feel a pressure, as if someone is on top of me, but it isn't nasty. When I talk, I get answers or what I think are answers, and sometimes I feel if I really concentrate I can see someone very faintly. For some reason I think I can always smell cinnamon.'

'When did you start feeling this then?'

'Well, for as long as I can remember really. Then when mum died it didn't happen, but this week when I went back to school.' Cameron took a sip of juice. He saw Emily was listening to him intently, so he felt the confidence to carry on. 'I felt the same pressure again this week. I was in the dormitory and Mr Abigail, that's my art teacher, was talking to me about my project, all around I could feel changing pressures, I don't really know the best way to explain it Emily.'

'I think I know what you mean Cameron, a lot of people believe the spirits of people, guardian angels and guides are all around us, all the time. Some people have a special talent and can communicate with them. Maybe you are receptive to them.' Emily got up from the table and stirred the rabbit casserole then looked at her watch. 'Sweet Mary, look at the time your father will be home any moment now.'

Cameron was left with his thoughts as the conversation ended abruptly. Emily disappeared into the dining room to lay the table ready for supper.

Cameron's father sensed a new sparkle in his son. He felt Cameron thinking, once again probing and questioning everything that surrounded him. Cameron chatted away, talking about school and Josh. He looked over at his father, sipping at a generous measure of his favourite brandy. Cameron thought his father looked tired. Sebastian had forgotten to take off his spectacles, a habit Cameron's mother always used to jibe him about. His long face and strong jaw held a days shadow of stubble. His father was an envoy extraordinary, as a professor of religious studies at Oxford University, specialising in religious fundamentalism, he had been recruited and assigned by the British government to assist all their ambassadors around the world in dealing with the ever emerging sensitivities of religious harmony and tolerance.

'I have to go away on Monday Cam' said Sebastian.

'Where are you going?' asked Cameron.

'Rome, I have already left all my contact details with your headmaster, and Emily. But if you need me for anything you can contact me on my mobile phone.'

Cameron nodded, he always thought his father's work was very glamorous, even though he did not actually know what he did, Cameron knew his father worked for the government and was sent all over the world. Sometimes at very short notice. It was at these times his mother would spend a lot of time and effort making sure she created an environment where Cameron was not affected by his father's long spells away. He could remember her not being very good at any of the sports, luckily his natural athletic ability shone through, rather than a dependence on her to hone any lacking proficiency.

'One day maybe I could come with you when you go away on business?'

His father replied enthusiastically 'that is a great idea Cam I would like that very much. If I have a trip planned the next time you have a school break then I cannot see a problem.'

His father's thoughts focused on Cameron's deep brown eyes, which complimented his Mediterranean complexion. An attribute he inherited from his mother. Sebastian saw the same warm gaze from the moment he had first met Rebecca; he was captivated with her from the very first moment he saw her. He swirled the brandy around in the glass, the house was colder without her presence, his thoughts filled with the memories he kept locked away, they were his memories, only his, unshared with anyone else.

'Sebastian would you like some fruit pie?' Emily took his brandy glass from him, refilling it with another large measure.

'That would be lovely Emily. Oh, where has Cam gone?' Sebastian deep in thought had not noticed Cameron leave the room.

'He went upstairs' Emily handed him the glass, 'he asked about Rebecca before you came home.'

Sebastian sat forward in the leather chair, after a small pause he replied 'did he, what did he ask?'

'He asked why she died, and things of the like.' The large Georgian rooms never allowed words to carry from one to another but Emily had lowered her voice instinctively.

Sebastian sat back into the chair, the silence loud with the rustle of his hand rubbing over the days growth of stubble on his chin. 'He seems a lot brighter since returning back to school, it has been along time. I have never heard him mention his mother at all since the funeral. He certainly hasn't said anything to me.' Sebastian slurped a large gulp of Brandy.

'He is a strong boy' said Emily, 'he holds his feelings deep inside. It would appear he is now beginning to try and find out the answers he needs to move forward.'

Sebastian crossed his legs, the last of the brandy drunk his thoughts returned to his wife.

Sariel looked down at Malach. The wound on the protector's arm was covered with a linen dressing. Malach was very pale, sweat beads collected on his bare chest and brow. The weapons of The Fallen legions came from the Fires of the Damned, any wound if not fatal would cast the victim into an abyss of pain. The only defence was for the body and mind to shut down, allowing healing to take place during an unconscious phase. Malach's eyes were closed yet moved rapidly, periodically one of his fingers would twitch.

'Has everything been done Seir?' asked Sariel, his tall frame stooping over the bed. The archangel stood upright and turned towards the healer angel, looking down at her small, fragile frame in stark contrast to his powerful stature.

'Yes, he is restless, the wound to his arm is very deep. It must have been complete torment when it was sustained. I sense a deep inner strength,' replied Seir looking up at Sariel.

'Quite' the archangel strode towards the door, he stopped and without turning said sharply. 'I want to know the moment the protector rises.'

'Of course, immediately sire' replied Seir. Sariel left to report back to his fellow council members.

Seir twisted round as she heard Malach whisper a few words, she could only make out the word Sam, but it was a sure sign the pain had started to ease. She thought it unusual a member of the Archangel Council was so interested in a protector's progress, Seir had been reporting to Sariel every change, or not, as Malach's progress had been slow. The archangel always received the information with regard, but at times would seem impatient at the length of time Malach's recovery was taking. Sariel and the Archangel Council would have to be patient, the protector was improving, but his recovery would demand more time.

Sariel found Michael looking across towards the two peaks, his broad shoulders seemingly supporting the weight of the growing concerns emanating from the protector's attack.

'The protector is improving Michael. The healer reckons it will not be much longer and the pain will have diminished entirely.'

'That is good.' Michael did not turn round, continuing to focus across the vast city and kingdom of the Enlightened.

'You are troubled?' enquired Sariel.

Michael frowned, he began to take slow considerate steps around the hall. 'The appearance of Samsaweel and it's connection with the boy. Serapiel is one of our most experienced consorts, we would be fools to throw away her insight with disregard. We are witnessing The Fallen increasing their pressure on man, we have seen a change in attitude towards the faith and guidance of the Highest Power over many moons.' His silence was punctuated by the drone of the falls, 'I sense a change Sariel. Similar, but far more sinister, to the senses we all had which led to the 2nd Battle of Zo-Har.'

'But what of the boy? Why does he fill our consciences so?'

Michael shook his head, 'I know not Sariel. The boy does seem to be growing larger in our consciences. Why? There have been many entities throughout time who have possessed the desire to communicate with us. But if Serapiel is correct and he also has the ability to throw down the barriers of his world and can see his protector.' Michael looked hard at Sariel 'and subsequently the kingdoms! Then that is very rare. The Fallen would do anything to gain the boy's faith, he would be extremely useful to them.'

As Cameron walked into his bedroom, the air pulsed, a pressure surrounded him. His senses were drawn towards the corner of his room, he walked over to his study table and switched on the lamp, within his bedroom the shadows formed. As he adjusted to the fading gloom of the room he thought he saw an outline, a tall figure standing in the corner that disappeared as the light came on. Cameron scratched his head, more to satisfy the itch inside rather than on the skin. He sniffed but this time no hint of cinnamon was forthcoming.

Don't be silly he thought. He became angry with himself, he had been questioning everything affecting his life and his feelings from the moment of his mother's death. Cameron had shut himself away in a self-protecting bubble. Nothing had mattered to him, the importance of school, exams, friendships and relationships were pushed to one side. The biggest change was the defensive wall he had built very rapidly to protect himself from anymore hurt, if he unattached himself from relationships which had meaning to him, he would not suffer if they are taken as his mum was. The grip of pain was no weaker now than it had been a year ago, when he stood by his father's side looking into the deep hole down at his mother's coffin. But now he began to feel a desire grow inside to seek the reasons of her death. It's purpose. This desire prised apart the bubble he had enveloped himself in. He wanted to know the truth.

Out of the shadows the daemon stalked, he felt the boy open his mind. How can anyone say mum going to heaven to be with God is right, Cameron thought. It hasn't been right for me, or dad, or even Emily for that matter. Emily said we all have a path, but what reason is there for mum's path to lead her to leave us. Cameron tapped a pencil in between his teeth rhythmically as his mind churned over and over. He stared at the ceiling, his body relaxing into his soft bed. Mr Abigail kept saying the angels were only interested in looking after themselves, if that isn't true how could they think by taking mum they were doing anything to look after me? How could they think that? Cameron felt a pressure to the side of him, he turned his head to see where it came from. His computer screen flickered as the screen saver changed, the lamp on his desk sent a downward glow over the far corner of his bedroom. He thought he saw the air pulse beside him, a quiver similar to the hot air from an opened oven.

The daemon stood by his bed, an opportunity was presenting itself. The boy was questioning the Enlightened.

This was his most vulnerable moment, the protective cocoon Cameron had put up around himself left him guarded against The Fallen as much as it did with Malach, was being prised apart.

If God loves us all why is there so many bad things that happen? Why do people do bad things to other people, how come he lets them do these things? Cameron grew frustrated at the questions churning through his mind, with no answers forthcoming. He shivered, a familiar gnawing pain brushed over him, Cameron curled up into a ball. The tears fell, pushed outwards as he closed his eyes, he drifted away into sleep with a stifled sob. A smirk grew on Jetrel's face, Samsaweel will be most pleased, his thoughts hung over Cameron as he melted into the shadows.

Seir vigorously mixed the green gloop which thickened into a smooth paste in the mortar, it's sweet aromatic smell increased as it reached just the right texture. Malach had grown weaker during the moments of his unconsciousness but his strength was gradually returning with Seir's meticulous attention. She would miss the protector when he returned to his duties, he had taken up a great deal of her time, attending to his wound followed by endless reporting to the Archangel Council. The council members kept a silence which intrigued her, she never had to report the condition of any wounded angel to any of the councils before, the protector's clash with a daemon in itself wasn't unusual so why the deep interest in his condition? Seir had grown fond of looking over Malach, although she wondered whether it was the protector himself or the attention of the council she found intriguing.

As she entered the room Seir found Malach sitting on

the side of his bed, rubbing the long wound on his forearm gently with his finger. His features were drawn, and he had an unhealthy grey pallor but she could see this belied a subtle handsomeness.

'Malach?' whispered Seir as she stepped into the room.

'Hello' Malach looked up, his eyes deep set and heavy. He gently smoothed his forearm with the palm of his hand.

'How are you feeling?' Seir asked. She knelt down beside him, gently taking his arm without permission. Malach stared into her eyes, deep blue, rich as the Sea of Souls he thought. As she leant forward, a wisp of brown hair fell down across her face. Malach pushed it to one side catching her cheek with the tip of his finger. He paused, feeling her soft skin. Seir instinctively jerked her head away, feeling embarrassed she had done so. She hadn't seen his hand move to push away the curl of hair, and was surprised by it, but wasn't upset he had touched her in such a tenderly manner. Seir now realised it would be the protector she missed rather than the attention of the archangels.

Malach unlocked his gaze, 'I cannot thank you enough Seir.'

'There is no thanks required Malach, this is my role,' she replied.

He was surprised how he felt slightly put out at the thought Seir was watching over him because it was her role rather than out of a deeper duty.

'Even so I am very grateful.'

Malach smiled at her, a smile Seir did not see as she very gently covered the wound with the aromatic paste.

'Your wound will require no more than this last covering, it has healed very quickly.'

Malach could not disguise his sense of disquiet at the possibility of leaving her in the near future. Seir stopped applying the paste, but continued to focus on the protector's arm even though she could feel Malach's deep gaze upon her.

'You don't have to leave though.' She said with a hint of embarrassment, concerned the protector may seen behind the veil of duty. 'The wound may have healed but your strength has to return, you will become tired very quickly.'

'Then I will trust you to return my strength with your kindness Seir.'

Once his wound was redressed Malach felt a need to escape the confines of the small room, he walked heavy footed upon the rich marbled pavements of the city. Crowds bustled around the stalls in the market. Angels bartering with jewellery makers, the linen weavers cutting pieces of cloth to their requested measurements. The traders of parchment haggled with scholars and musicians whilst they picked through the stalls. Musical notes played out of sequence on instruments, echoed around the market in stark contrast to the splendour of the choir voices which drifted across the Sea of Souls from the seven palaces far on the horizon.

He stood and stared into the crystal clear waters of one of the four fountains which sat in the four corners of the large market square, weariness gripped his body. Each fountain's centre piece was a huge white marbled unicorn, which sat in the middle of sprouting petalled shaped water. Malach would increase the length of his daily walks as his strength allowed, but his frustration grew as he became more and more impatient to return to Cameron; but he knew Seir was right to keep him from rushing back to his side.

'It is good to see you up and about Malach.'

He turned to see Serapiel smiling back at him.

'Hello Serapiel, it is very good to see you.'

Malach sat on the edge of the fountain wall, Serapiel flicked her purple cloak from underneath her and joined him.

'Your strength returns?'

'Yes, too slowly though. Seir says it might be a few more earth moons before I can return to...' Malach paused and looked across the square towards the seven palaces in the far distance.

'It is better you return to your entity with your strength re-grown Malach, Cameron will need you revitalised, not weak and needing a wall for support.' Serapiel softly smiled at him her eyes warm. 'When you do return Malach be on your guard,' Serapiel saw Malach attempt to sit straighter, the tips of his wings flickered as he pushed his chest out. 'The Fallen will have taken the time you have been away from the boy to seek out and assess his strength, his desire to either keep his path to the Enlightened strong, or....'

Malach stood, a well of anger, a pool of desired revenge echoed in his voice. 'The Fallen, when I return, will never get to Cameron again.'

'The boys path is something you cannot directly control Malach. The path is to be chosen by the boy. We, you, can guide and do what is necessary to protect him from The Fallen, but if an entity is determined they will yield.'

Her hand caressed the cool waters of the fountain, the sounds of activity throughout the market had drifted from Malach as he listened intently to his consort. 'In all but a few entities the light never truly dims, for some the dark leads them to achieve their trail of melancholy; then when they are finished they leave them to find the path of Enlightenment again. The turmoil created left to fester the work of The Fallen.'

As Malach rejoined Serapiel back on the fountain wall, she placed her hand on his covered forearm.

'The protector must be there to guide them. It is the moment when a protector needs to be at his strongest.'

Samsaweel stretched his wings wide in satisfaction. Unlike the angels of the Enlightened, whose wings were tipped with colour dependent on status and role, The Fallen angel's wings were all white tipped with black, apart from Lucifer, who had wings as black as the rock which lined the Fires of the Damned. Jetrel stood before the archangel, confident in Samsaweel's pleasure at hearing Cameron was at last appearing to weaken.

At last, an opening has presented itself. Samsaweel was relieved he would have something positive to report to Lucifer when called upon. This opportunity must not be wasted, the consequences would not be pleasant, Samsaweel shuddered at the thought of Lucifer's wrath.

'You have done well.'

The dark archangel peered through the small window of his antechamber across the great hall. A fire crackled in the corner of his room, adding light to the gloomy dark which the orbs of light on the wall struggled to dispel.

'I do not want you to leave the boy again, not even to report back to me. I will summon you. Until that moment every break in the boy's resolve has to be exploited. Do you understand?'

Jetrel bowed.

'His protector will eventually return, when he does…..' Samsaweel clasped his hands together, narrowed his eyes. 'Destroy him!'

Chapter Three

Sebastian pulled the neck of his heavy coat tighter as the chilled wind blew from the River Tiber across the massed crowd in St Peters Square. He looked down the recently erected platform which swayed underfoot, at the gathered line of government representatives, most of the faces he recognised. A few from newly elected powers were unknown to him. A polite nod here and there would break the ice, a more formal meeting would be made at the evening reception. Sebastian noted the entrance of the papal nuncio, the pope's envoy walked along the line of dignitaries, shaking each one's hand in turn. Sebastian watched as he approached, thinking how typically Roman he looked. Tall, statuesque physique hidden beneath a long, black coat, the papacy coat of arms visible on the left breast. His olive complexion giving him a healthy pallor. The nuncio's large nose the focal point of his features. He greeted the British Ambassador courteously, then reached out and shook Sebastian's hand warmly as he stood. The two men had worked closely together over the five years of Pope Steven's papal reign. The nuncio took a seat at the end of the platform, the gathered now awaited the imminent arrival of the Pope.

The Swiss Guard resplendent in their distinctive Medici blue, red and yellow uniforms stood to attention. The Halberdiers red ostrich feathered plumes atop their Morion helmets fluttered, whilst their Halberds gleamed in the low winter sun. The honour guard formed a protective corridor from the entrance of the Papal Palace sitting high on the Vaticanus Mons, the lines parted as they reached the raised lectern. Pope Steven appeared. A cheer rose, rippling away from the platform as the front rows of the massed crowd saw him first. He slowly but purposefully walked towards the lectern, raising his hand to the crowd, silence fell across St Peters Square.

'It is the duty of all men,' he began 'to look within themselves for the choices that will direct us all towards peace in the world. The dreams of peace and prosperity for all can be a reality. Faiths are not exclusive realms of belief, all faiths must come together, they must lead the way forward. It isn't enough for protectionism which is singularly biased; to the detriment of the symbol of faith in whatever form it takes. The people of this world, where the trinkets of wealth and celebrity are coveted by the masses, need to be shown their dedication towards the light is not taken for granted by the messengers of God's word.'

He paused as he turned over the page of his speech, he purposefully scanned the masses, then continued.

'In a troubled world where nations have the ability to eradicate hopelessness and perpetuate optimism and aspiration, I call upon all leaders both religious and…..'

Heavy, grey clouds sailed across the Italian capital, before it a sombre gloom cloaked the Vatican City. From the raised platform Sebastian saw the curtain of sleet move ever closer. It was a strangely bleak day he thought. Pope Steven paused, the crowd and invited dignitaries waited.

Suddenly his legs buckled, slumping him over the lectern. A small trickle of blood appeared from below his

Mitre following the contours of his brow. His eyes stared far away into the distance, to a place where the living could not reach. A purr of confusion emanated from the front rows of spectators, rising into an hysterical roar as the realisation of what had just occurred dawned upon them.

A tall member of the Swiss Guard stepped up onto the platform approaching the still body of the Pope. As he reached the Pontiff, his throat was ripped open by a bullet from an unseen assassin. The Halberdier made a futile attempt to cover the gaping wound, the blood gushed through his fingers, it was a forlorn attempt to stem the flow. His face turned from a vibrant flushed pink to a deathly pallor as the life drained from within. His body slammed to the floor of the platform, screams and panic fell over the crowd, and assembled officials.

Sebastian fell to his knees as all around him confusion and terror gripped the dignitaries, the British Ambassador joined him in wide eyed incomprehension. Sebastian noted the Swiss Guard's blood speckled across the Ambassador's face and across the front of his grey coat. Their eyes met, the Ambassador shook his head, no words were needed.

Upon Michael's return from the summoned meeting of The Collective, he sent his herald to request the presence of his fellow councillors. They entered the hall to find Michael sitting on the council throne, his pensive thoughts evident. The thrum of the Falls of the Divine enveloped the chamber.

'Your herald asked us to join you here immediately Michael.' Gabriel stood below the dais with his arms tucked behind his back under his wings, his lapis blue cloak hanging awkwardly.

'Yes' Michael looked grim. 'Yes, thank you for coming so readily.'

The six archangels focused hard on Michael, his manner demanded it.

'A Bridge-Maker has been slain!'

Michael's fellow council members looked around at each other, the assassination of a Bridge-Maker was not unusual but rare. The leaders of man's religious unions were seen as untouchable, despite the huge chasm in opinion of individuals reliance in faith.

'The ramifications of the Bridge-Makers death may extend very wide. There will certainly be deep consternation. The Principality Council have sent forth their commanders to seek the cause, we have to be alert to the fact there maybe something more sinister about this killing than human notoriety' asserted Michael.

'It is unknown for a Bridge-Maker to be targeted in recent times' said Uriel, 'but what information is there that would suggest this was more than an entity seeking infamy.'

'The concern Uriel, is no-one has foreseen an attack on the Bridge-Maker nor has any of the councils had any information which may lead to a deeper issue…..'

'But?' interrupted Raphael.

Michael disappointedly replied. 'There is not really a but Raphael, there isn't really any definitive explanation to suggest we should be concerned about the killing of the Bridge Maker.' Michael narrowed his eyes, his mind questioning the concerns he had but not outwardly showing his peers, not yet at least.

'But as we have seen' said Raphael 'the attacks on the protectors has increased markedly, we are seeing attempts on them increase with The Fallen becoming ever bolder, maybe bold enough to strike out at a Bridge Maker.'

Gabriel agreed. 'The pattern has changed. The Fallen would, given the opportunity, seek to take the light from a protector. Although recently they have actively hunted the opportunity to claim the protector's aleph!'

Michael nodded his head in acknowledgement.

'It is a point which has not gone unnoticed Gabriel.'

A few hours following the assassination of Pope Steven, Sebastian sat before the Ambassador and his entourage; the death of the Pontiff would create an international incident. His killer was still at large, no fundamentalist group had yet claimed responsibility. The high profile assassination would be the catalyst to a news frenzy focused on the possible cause or struggle.

'Who did it gentlemen?'

The Ambassador sat behind a large dark oak table, the extraordinarily large room within the Papal Palace had been allocated to them when the Vatican City was sealed off by the Swiss Guard, supported by a further outer ring by the Italian police force and army. It was an open ended question, he did not believe at this stage any of his staff would know who had fired the gun, it was suggestions he needed, brainstorming.

The Ambassador's deputy spoke first. 'The attack was too professional to be just a madman who got lucky sir. Firstly, the shot, just one straight through the Pope's head. Secondly, it was from a specialised gun, not one which could be used by someone off the street. Third, he or she hasn't been caught, suggesting they had an escape route pre-planned.'

The Ambassador sat back in the leather chair, his elbows on the padded arms, a forefinger resting against his front teeth. 'Motives?'

Sebastian sat forward, 'If I may sir.'

The Ambassador nodded.

'Pope Steven was seen as a radical. He is the first Pope ever to stand against the established theological strands of all faiths. He questioned. He was unpopular amongst some religious and political leaders.'

'Sebastian you are not suggesting …'

'Sir, I am not suggesting anything. Just presenting an insight into the man and the particular issues his style of leadership has brought about.'

'Yes, of course.'

The Ambassador looked pensive and troubled. A thoughtful silence echoed around the flamboyantly painted room.

'The consequences gentlemen, if it transpires this tragedy has been borne out of an order from either a religious or political leader, are too dire to contemplate.'

Lucifer's voice rose in intensity as his pleasure grew at the news that the Bridge-Maker's life had been taken.

'The world has been sent a wonderful message, no matter who you are or what you think or believe…….it means nothing!'

Dalkiel skulked behind the dark prince, smirking and wringing his hands in pleasure. His ragged wings fluttered uncontrollably at his master's pleasure. Lucifer paid no attention to his councillor shifting amongst the shadows. A place where Dalkiel felt comfortable.

'I hear the plans to move towards the angel kingdom are

going well Zaebos.'

'They are my prince,' the burly count bowed whilst searching for Dalkiel amongst the shadows. 'Your councillor has been kept fully informed of all the issues.'

Lucifer stepped down from the dais, he slowly, menacingly stood tall looking down at his chiefs and commanders. Lucifer's smooth features gave away no hint to his inner thoughts as the summoned throng moved out of the way from his path. Dalkiel stepped from the shadows into the dim light of the hall.

'I have been keeping a close eye on the proceedings my lord.'

Dalkiel received narrowed eyed stares from Dagon and Zaebos.

Lucifer did not turn to face his councillor. 'Well I know who to seek if there is any failure!' he said in a low menacing whisper, loud enough for all to hear, especially Dalkiel. Dagon smirked as he watched the councillor tentatively step back into the shadows of the hall.

The great doors of the hall opened, the in rush of air from the passageway caused the fug of smoke high in the vaults of the ceiling to swirl frantically. The Daemon Chief, Abelech entered, his black cloak almost horizontal, flapping as it struggled against his powerful strides.

'Ah Abelech, well we welcome your presence. Your lateness will be overlooked this time,' Lucifer returned to his throne 'you have done well, what news do you bring?'

Abelech approached the dais, acknowledging Lucifer with a bow. He was a clever angel, able to quickly sum up the strengths and weaknesses of other angels upon a first meeting. He had a quick mind, he had to have. The work of the daemons was a vast and complex business. He greeted the presence of Zaebos and Dagon with a tip of his head.

'The Bridge-Maker's slaying will be associated with man's religious factions. Man is as weak as he as ever been, as they have done since the first dawn they squabble and fight each other. Whereas in the past their cause had meaning, a call which rallied the masses towards it; minorities now proceed to go round in circles and become ever more entrenched in their own separate idealistic views. Whilst the masses are happy to go about with their insular existence, wishing to push aside the scenes of despair that walk within their world,' Abelech paused, turning towards the assembled leaders of The Fallen, 'they are unable to fall on their swords and compromise, we have many daemons in place, some are with the leaders of both their nations and their so-called faiths.'

Lucifer revelled in the welcomed news.

'Excellent Abelech! It is the beginning of a dawn which will once again send the Enlightened scurrying to man's side. The boy will be far from their sights. The Enlightened are strong, we have seen their ability to strengthen man's resolve. Our recent energies brought about their two huge conflicts, it caused every nation to pour their resources into the destruction of one another; we almost succeeded in bringing man to their knees.'

Lucifer paused, his stare focused on a point far into the distance.

'We have not the time to commence a war of man based on empire, land or resource. Abelech you have struck the first sword into the heart of man's downfall and that of the cursed Aleph! Man's imbecilic devotion to faith will be exploited, the boy's attention will be focused to the futile worth of piety.'

The assembled leaders of The Fallen revelled in the miasma of the great hall, before Lucifer sent them to begin the next phase.

Cameron had been informed by his headmaster of the news from Rome during the day. The news of his father's safety amongst all the confusion swirling around his mind was a relief, but he had found it difficult to concentrate on his studies. His father's return from Rome would be delayed, but he would return home, a fact Cameron pondered on as he lay in his bed looking up at the ceiling. He could hear Josh on his bed reading from a book, mumbling the words under his breath, as he usually did. It was a trait which despite repeated protestations from teachers and fellow pupils alike, remained.

Cameron blanked it out as his thoughts were full of the events in Rome. He had spent the whole evening in the common room watching the news which was minute by minute analysis of the assassination. *I don't understand why he would allow someone to kill the Pope? It cannot be right he would just do nothing!*

'You are right, what merciful God would allow these things to happen? You are correct to doubt, embrace those thoughts, they will guide you to the real and true path.' Jetrel flicked his cloak from under him as he sat on the edge of Josh's bed. Josh continued to mumble. Jetrel continued to press home the spread of discontent. 'What kind of God allows his so called power to be flouted. A weak, pointless one!'

Cameron heard the words. Words that mingled with the questions filling his conscience, words which appeared through his confusion. His eyes grew heavier, his world blurred and he was carried through into the vision of his dream.

The old man scribbled frantically, the sharp edge of the feather scratching away at the parchment. A dip into the small metal pot of ink, a click as he tapped off the excess, then the words flowed again. A shaft of sunlight speared through the small open window, a corner of the top finished parchment which sat on the pile others lifted as a fresh breath of air rushed into the room, it went unnoticed. The old man turned the pages of a large heavy book, he read for a few moments, sat back in his chair and rubbed his eyes. He thoughtfully glanced out of the window then returned to his scribbling.

Cameron twitched, and pulled his quilt over his shoulders unconsciously shutting out the chill of the night air.

The old man was interrupted by a knock on the door, he blew hard on the written wet ink, lifted the parchment, wafting it around in front of him. Placing a gentle forefinger on the last word he wrote to make sure the ink was dry enough, he placed it upside down on the pile. He snapped the book shut and beckoned the person outside to enter. The door slowly opened, a small man appeared, he walked over to the table and placed a metal plate with a chunk of bread and slices of meat on it next to the old man, then placed a fresh decanter of wine on the window sill, after a few exchanged words the small man bowed and left. The old man cut a slice of bread, and washed it down with small sips of wine, he once again began to read the elaborate lettering on the heavily foxed pages within the large book, as he read he turned the pages which were delicately crisp and chipped with extreme age.

The daemon converged his mind onto the chink of image emerging from Cameron's. Jetrel saw what he thought was a window, an old window with squares of stain glass present, it was faint, too faint to be sure, then what appeared to be a man hunched over something. He shook his head in frustration as he struggled to see any clearer. Whilst the boy had shown a change of direction, albeit it questioningly, towards the dark, this did allow Jetrel to tentatively scan his dreams. But Cameron's belief in the path of The Fallen would need to be far stronger for Jetrel to see the images more clearly. Samsaweel will be very satisfied with the progress he thought, he knew the images would remain blurred so he backed away into the gloom of the night.

Cameron stirred, rubbing his eyes as he sat up in bed. Through his sleepy state he felt the familiar pressure about him. He blinked his heavy eyes slowly. What was the book? he thought. The words weren't English, the dream has never gone that far before. The dormitory was now full of sleeping boys, he looked across at Josh who had fallen asleep reading. His bedside light was still on, the book hung precariously over the side of the bed, gripped tight by his fingers. He lay back down and allowed a puzzled sleep state to return. Cameron slept, the dream could wait until the morning.

The stern features of the Ambassador concerned Sebastian. Sebastian, along with the other members of the Embassy staff who had been kept within the Vatican City following the assassination of Pope Steven, had been summoned to his office. News about the killing surely thought Sebastian, by the looks of it, the news is not good.

'Thank you for coming so promptly at this late hour gentleman', the Ambassador in turn looked directly at each face in the room before he continued. 'I wanted to give you the updated news which I have received from the papal nuncio, before you heard it through the media. A body has been discovered on the outskirts of the city. A note accompanied the body claiming the assassination of the Pope was by a radical faction which at present has declined to name themselves. Worryingly it states the targeting of the Pope was only one of a series of killings which will be aimed at all heretic figures who promote the apostasy of faith.'

A pensive hush fell across the room.

'Is there any further news on the faction sir?' Sebastian asked.

'No, unfortunately not, it claims more information will be released as it carries out the calling of the higher faith. Gentleman I do not need to tell you the ramifications of not only the discovery of this note regarding the murder of Pope Steven; but the deeper consequences, if it is true they are targeting other religious leaders, the stability of certain areas of the world is in question. The urgency of finding out who is actually behind this group is vital.'

'Sir, the body, does it give any clues to the nature of the group?'

The Ambassador thumbed through the report on his desk.

'No, it doesn't, there is a post mortem taking place to ascertain the cause of death. There is no description as yet, I suppose we will have to wait for that information to filter through.'

'I suppose the chances of working on any leads to find

the whereabouts of this group, or the ring leaders are frankly very remote?' Sebastian continued with a sobering tone, 'we may have to wait until they, whoever they may be, move again!'

As Malach walked along the city wall towards the tower on the Gate of Arabah, he looked towards the two peaks. The magnificent snow tipped mountains sat at the far edge of the lands of the Enlightened, the vast Forest of Wandering Spirits stretching along the foot of the mountains. The protector watched as lights danced through the branches and around the strong tree trunks. The forest held the flickering lights of souls waiting for their return to the world of entities. As each soul was called into the world, the lights shot up out of the forest canopy, leaving a sparkling tail of iridescent light in their wake. They disappeared into the sky towards the top of the mountains, fading as their light brightened on the other side of the peaks.

He took a deep breath, stretching his wings the protector paused resting against the walled parapet. The lush green pastures were broken into slices of land as the small tributaries fingered they way from the River Nephesh. Flocks of birds winged their way just above the water, settling on the edges of the soft banks. The air held a hint of aromatic blossom.

His strength had returned. He would return to Cameron when he next slept. The protector continued to walk towards the tower, as he drew nearer the sentry turned, Malach sensed a frown brood across his forehead underneath his highly embellished golden helmet.

'You are not permitted to walk the wall unless you have

permission from the Captain of the watch. I take it you have such permission?' snapped the guard.

Malach knew the rules, he had managed to slip past the guard at the bottom of the steps, wanting to see the panoramic view of the landscape beyond the city wall.

'Erm......no I haven't got permission. I will leave straight away, I just wanted to get a good look at the kingdom before I return to my entity. A little while ago I nearly never got to see this sight again.'

Malach lifted his forearm. The wound was fully healed, but the scar would be there forever.

The soldier glanced at Malach's arm, 'a run in with the dark?'

'Yes, although he came off a lot worse' Malach said pulling back his shoulders.

'Seems you were fortunate, many protectors have recently had the light taken from them.'

Malach nodded in acknowledgement, rumours were beginning to spread throughout the angel kingdom of the increasing attacks of The Fallen. The road below thronged with the comings and goings of angels going about their angelic duty. Protectors returning from their duties, seeking the advice of their consorts, or the audience of the councils in their quest to serve their entity. Angels of the Principalities going about their tasks of guiding the leaders of nations and all mans self made individualistic faiths. The Thrones responding to the request from protectors and principals, carrying out the 'miracles' which enhanced the path of an entity or nation, but always balancing out their role and actions with the sacred words of the scrolls.

Malach looked up at the soldier, 'well I had better go, I don't want to get us both into any trouble by being here.

Thanks for not throwing me off at the first opportunity.'

The soldier veiled a smile back and gestured his head back towards the stairs from the wall 'be off.'

Malach left the kingdom behind through the north gate, the feelings of relief in finally being able to return to his entity were tinged with a heaviness at leaving the kingdom behind and Seir. He promised her he would visit her as soon as it was necessary to return back to the city. The image of her tearful blue eyes had finally stirred within him the feelings he now realised he had been suppressing, but the duty of a protector was to their entity alone. He had vowed never to allow anything to get in the way of this but, the call of duty was now accompanied by a new sensation for Seir. Malach revelled in it's ability to reach deep within him, but he pushed the feelings aside. Unsure of the dangers he was walking back into, he would need all of his senses unclouded and focused.

Whilst he had been recuperating the protector had come to appreciate the beauty of the angel kingdom, he had never had the time or the opportunity to absorb it's magnificence before. His visits had always been hurried, normally on official business relating to his duties. He now passed through the Forest of Wandering Spirits; listening, he always marvelled at the birdsong, loud and clear unlike the tainted song in the world of entities, he never enjoyed the noise of living that dulled the natural sounds. The forest was a hive of activity. The path leading to the conduit was always a bustling highway, but within the forest itself the throng of life was evident.

The breeze kissed the canopies high above making the trees shiver. Leaves floated from the branches, gently dancing their way to the ground; enjoying their fleeting moment of freedom. Malach passed a couple of badgers preening themselves in the warm air, their cub snuffled loudly amongst the shrubs occupying the forest floor. His attention was suddenly drawn to a movement in the distance. A shadow stopped, tensed as the realisation it had been seen instinctively tightening it's muscles. Malach was sure it was a small deer, he stopped and tried to peer through the dense undergrowth. In an instant it had gone, disappearing to the safety of the deep forest. He smiled and continued towards the conduit.

As the protector emerged from the other side, a short distance in front of him stood the conduit. Two enormous angel wings carved into either side of the mountains marked the entrance and exit to the angel kingdom and the world of entities. A small garrison was situated next to the conduit, The Powers guarding the kingdom against any unwanted visitors. Malach drew nearer, the sound of the falls growing in intensity. He felt a sense of excitement at returning to Cameron's side, for him it had been a very long, frustrating time. His duty would not be interrupted by The Fallen again. The gateway of the conduit was heaving with the comings and goings of angels, Malach joined the queue looking for the reason behind the delay. Ahead he could see a group of soldiers fussing around at the entrance; he thought the chaotic scene was an ideal smoke screen for any servant of The Fallen to make a hidden bid to access the conduit rather than a strong deterrent. The line moved forward and he was soon the attention of a young looking soldier whose irritation at the constant haranguing of his officers was borne out upon the protector.

'Your business, state your business! Hurry!'

'I...I am on my way to my entity. I am Malach, protector...'

'Yes! Yes! I can see you are a protector...' the soldier snapped 'your business, why have you been within the city?'

Malach struggled to hear him as the frustration of angels returning and leaving increased in a noisy torrent. 'I have been injured...' he replied raising his voice at the same time as his arm. The soldier glanced at the long scar down his forearm 'I am now returning to...'

'Yes, ok move on!'

Malach glared at the soldier angrily, put out by his obvious indifference.

He stepped forward, just managed to spread his wings and launched down the face of the falls. The power and noise of the water overwhelmed him, despite the many occasions he had used the conduit he never dulled of it's magnificence. He fell further, the angels accompanying him faded as they went upon their own individual quests. The sound of the falls dimmed as he neared the edge of the angelic partition. The light around him dimmed, a sign he was returning at night. He swept his wings back and surged forward, breaking through into a moonlit sky, far below he could see the small silver disk that was Crawford Lake. The landscape was covered in a lunar shadow, the school only visible by the outline of spot lights that lit up the building.

Slow heavy breaths drifted through Cameron's dormitory, he was in a deep sleep, his scruffy hair poked out from under the duvet, the pillow squashed up against the headrest not needed as the mattress supported his head at an awkward angle. Malach smiled, it was good to be back, back for good he thought. He rubbed the scar on his arm, closed his eyes and joined Cameron's dream. Malach shivered. The Fallen had been with Cameron whilst he had been away, he sensed the cold foreboding that enclosed around the boy's thoughts. The images misted, he attempted to clear them, concentrating hard on prying through the veil of disbelief which had grown inside his entity.

With a deep sigh Malach rested his mind, he knew for now it was pointless trying to break through. Any entity which did not want to see the path of an angel, hindered them from accompanying them in their journey. The Fallen knew this as did the Enlightened. The plans The Fallen were laying down to bring the boy over to their path was the only way to see into his mind. Malach realised Cameron had begun to seriously question the light, he was not surprised; without his guidance and winged cloak to envelope him, protecting him from the attentions of the dark, the boy was slowly succumbing just as Samsaweel had predicted.

Malach returned to the words spoken by his consort, Cameron wasn't like any other fourteen year old boy, he is unlike most well above his years. I will be patient, I am here now, I will not fail him!

Malach stood in the corner of the room, partially hidden by it's shadows. He felt Jetrel approach just before the air swirled in the far corner and the dark angel stepped forward. Malach instantly noticed Jetrel was prepared, holding the hilt of his sword tightly.

'You have no place here. Turn around, leave the boy

alone!' Malach said firmly.

'I think it is you who should go protector. Leave now and you may return to the kingdom of deceivers; stay and I will extinguish the light from within you!' replied Jetrel confidently.

Malach knew the words meant nothing, he would not be allowed to leave even if he had any desire to. He hadn't and prepared himself to fight. The wound on his arm burnt, he swallowed hard at the thought of feeling the pain of a dark angel's sword again, Malach conscious of not showing any signs of weakness tried to block it out.

He drew his sword, the light from the shaft radiated a brilliant glow in the dark room.

'The last daemon to stand against me faltered. You will share his fate.'

'My dear Malach when I have finished with you, I will make sure it is the pain from my blade that grips the light throughout your body. I will make certain your end is slow, then the boy will be mine!'

Malach surged forward, he feinted a blow to the head of the daemon, lifting his sword above his head then twisting the thrust towards Jetrel's hip. Malach hoped the sudden rush at the daemon would catch him off guard but Jetrel easily parried the blade away.

'Is that it light-giver?' Jetrel taunted.

Malach ignored him, lunging forward again. His blade was again parried away to the side. Jetrel stayed on his back foot allowing Malach to attack, avoiding his sword with the skilfully timed movement of his body. The two angels danced around the dormitory, through the furniture and beds of the sleeping boys. Jetrel turned his shoulder away from another assault, but this time the dark angel pounced back. Malach just stopped the dark sword biting into his shoulder with the flick of his wrist, the two angels locked together. A test of strength proved each of them to be evenly matched, although Jetrel was sure he could sense Malach tiring. He pushed Malach as hard has he could, the protector lurched backwards disappearing through the dormitory wall out onto the hallway landing. Jetrel skipped through the wall after him, as he appeared Malach had regained his balance and was diving at him in another onslaught. With a flick of his wings, the protector launched himself at the daemon, a determined grimace etched across his face. Jetrel seeing it just in time, weaved back half way through the wall, he lifted his arm and with all the power he possessed he brought the butt of his sword pommel down square on top of Malach's head as the disappearing dark angel made him jerk forward exposing him to the powerful blow. Malach fell, he did not rise again.

Chapter Four

Samsaweel leant against the cold wall, his arms folded nonchalantly. Well how the mighty fall he thought, a chuckle resonating in his head. Malach lay where he was roughly thrown and chained, he remained unconscious. Samsaweel grew impatient. If he does not stir soon I will aid his recovery, he thought. I wish to pay my regards before Lucifer has his will. Irritated, Samsaweel left leaving instructions with the guard that he was to be notified the instant Malach showed signs of stirring.

As the archangel walked back through the interlinked network of corridors connecting the living quadrants of The Fallen city, he met Dalkiel.

'Ah Samsaweel there you are.'

'Councillor?'

'Zaebos would like to see you immediately' informed Dalkiel.

Samsaweel nodded, strange he thought the Machiavellian doing the bidding of the Grand Count. Dalkiel has obviously come along personally to gain his own information about our captive. Samsaweel keeping Dalkiel's nickname amongst The Fallen, to himself, followed Lucifer's councillor.

The two dark angels walked along the winding passageways, an uneasy silence was broken by Dalkiel, 'has the Enlightened one stirred?' he asked trying to sound as uninterested as he could possibly manage.

'No he has not, it would seem he was hit very hard' replied Samsaweel.

Dalkiel disappointed at the news enquired 'I take it he will recover?'

'Yes...' Samsaweel paused 'for now.'

'Quite' responded Dalkiel knowingly. His master would delight in the agony of one of the Enlightened. No doubt a prolonged event for the benefit of the city at large.

An uncomfortable Samsaweel was accompanied all the way to the great hall by Dalkiel, an unerring silence maintained, more so by the archangel, not wishing to enter into any conversation that could lead to the unwanted attention of Lucifer.

They now stood in front of the dais, unaware of their presence, Zaebos sat on the Throne of Azazel lost in his thoughts. They waited patiently, both knew it could be very painful if they disturbed the Grand Count not knowing what mood he was in until he spoke. Samsaweel saw Lucifer's councillor fidget with irritation at being made to wait. He smirked. Suddenly the great doors opened behind them, Dagon and Abelech entered the hall followed closely by Beleth, Bernael and Ertrael.

Zaebos shifted from his thoughts. Samsaweel now realised he had seen the two of them standing there, but was waiting for all the requested angels to arrive. Dalkiel was furious, but without Lucifer's presence would not show any sign of displeasure.

'Samsaweel.'

'My Lord?' replied Samsaweel bowing.

'How is our guest?'

'He has not yet stirred my Lord.'

'Hmm well we will wait, it isn't as if he is going

anywhere' Zaebos laughed. 'I take it the daemon is back with the boy?'

'Yes, he has returned. He is fully aware of the task that is required of him.'

'That is good, be sure to keep a very close eye on proceedings archangel. Report to Abelech or myself all that is reported back to you,' with a wave of his hand Samsaweel knew he was finished with and stepped to one side.

'Lucifer wants the protector alive!' Zaebos watched as the assembled group turned and looked at each other.

Dalkiel was the first to speak. 'Alive my Lord?' his tone betraying his outrage of being unaware of the dark prince's plans.

'Yes Dalkiel, alive!' Zaebos replied contemptuously. 'Lucifer wants the protector treated with care, his plan is to try and bring him within our fold. If we fail to achieve it, no matter. We will get the information we need out of him and then take the light from him.'

'What is Lucifer hoping to achieve by keeping the protector alive?'

'Do you not know Dalkiel?' asked Abelech tauntingly.

Dalkiel only had the time to glare up at Abelech.

Zaebos stood, 'the information we receive from within the angel kingdom is very sparse. Our informant within the walls has to be extremely cautious when contacting us. Their mission, thus far has been a success. The Enlightened have no idea of the importance of the boy to their ultimate downfall. If the protector proves to be susceptible to, how shall we say, our charms. Then it may be possible to place another traitor within the kingdom of light.'

Two flickering orbs of light sat in gargoyled beckets on the far side of the large cubed room, illuminating it in dancing light. The ominous lack of a door did not go unnoticed as Malach gazed around, trying to blink away the heavy blur. He tenderly felt the back of his head, his fingers slowly feeling a large bump as he parted his hair.

Where am I?

He attempted to stand, the chain connected to his ankle clanked as it ran along the floor. It was just long enough to allow him to walk gingerly into the middle of the room, then unsteadily back again to the welcomed support of the wall. A desperate grip of emotion clawed through him; whilst the dark angel had obviously not killed him, he realised this outcome may well be infinitely far worse. His wings quivered, he had left Cameron once again exposed to The Fallen. Guilt and failure ebbed through him. Malach slapped the wall hard leaning against it with his head resting on his forearms.

The protector sat in the corner of the room, his knees up against his chest with his wings wrapped around him. Lost in thoughtful despair, he had never heard of anyone being taken by The Fallen; the consequence of this was surely that no-one had ever lived to tell anyone about it. The fate of Cameron was uppermost in his mind, the boy was his first entity and he had failed him. Malach gripped his knees tighter to his chest, Serapiel's words churned over in his mind, 'When you return Malach be on your guard... The Fallen will have taken the time you have been away from the boy to seek out and assess his strength... The protector must be there to guide them. It is the moment when a protector needs to be at his strongest.' He rested his head back on the wall, not so long ago he was standing on the wall of the angel kingdom watching the birds glide over the

River Nephesh, in the distance he could see the Forest of Wandering Spirits. Malach brought his head down to rest on his knees, closed his eyes and tried to block everything out. It wasn't worth remembering memories that would ultimately fade, never to be seen again.

Malach opened his eyes.

Startled he jumped, there in front of him stood the most magnificent angel he had ever seen. Lucifer smiled. Malach stood, clawing his way up the wall needing it's support. Malach drawn by Lucifer's eyes, as black as his wings, awestruck by the vision of power that stood before him.

The dark prince bowed keeping his eyes focused on the protector, 'Malach, let me apologise for not being the perfect host' he said with a strong resonating voice.

The protector did not answer or return the bow, he tried to push himself deeper into the wall. Lucifer paced up and down, waiting to see if Malach would reply, assessing his quarry.

'I hope you can understand our need to be cautious. We will try and make things a lot more comfortable for you as soon as we can ascertain you will not be a threat.'

Malach still did not answer, he tried to weigh up his 'host'. Expecting a slow, painful death, here he was getting apologies.

'Hmmm well I can see you have things on your mind at the moment protector, it is to be expected.' Lucifer stepped closer to Malach. Malach froze. 'I will return later.' Lucifer turned and disappeared through a swirl of air in the wall.

The cool mists rolled from the hills of St Thomas and St Martins, settling in the valley of the Stour. The great spires of the cathedral towered over the city of Canterbury. From a distance the large building appeared strangely out of proportion to the surrounding countryside. Small unseen breaks in the cloud allowed the rays of the sun to probe through, illuminating fortunate sections of the Kentish landscape.

The Archbishop looked down upon the assembled congregation. Canterbury Cathedral full, as was usual on a Sunday, with a varied slice of the local population and the odd tourist all gathered listening to his sermon. He stood in the gothic styled pulpit, which complemented the feel of the nave with its towering vaulted ceilings; his words echoed through the vast medieval building, now in this modern day assisted by a microphone. His prayers for the slain Catholic pope were received. The hypnotic tones of the choir began to ebb throughout the cathedral drifting out into the great cloisters, and high into the beautiful fan vaulting of the Bell Harry Tower. Outside the winters day had an edge of spring about it. The soft smell of a new season lingered in the air. Groups of tourists walked around the perimeter of the building, cameras clicking, fingers pointing skyward at some point of interest. To the east of the cathedral a large group of french students huddled close together, looking in unison at different sections of the cathedral's structure on the instructions of their guide. Canterbury Cathedral had witnessed the Sabbath transformed over the years, many still held the deep respect for the religious meaning of the day of rest, but society at large had begun to walk away from the long held beliefs behind the rituals of a Sunday. The city centre began to fill with shoppers and tourists.

A white hot flash followed by an instant rippling thunderous explosion within the cathedral blew large segments of it's walls into the tourists milling around the perimeter. Inside, all those near to the epicentre of the bomb were vaporised, anyone not killed by the immediate explosion were subject to a barrage of flying debris and falling superstructure. The imposing cathedral tower faltered, as if a forlorn, invisible hand attempted to grasp the top of it; the tower swayed, then the pull of gravity dragged it slowly earthwards. Dust and smoke billowed through the narrow medieval streets, shoppers choked, panic stricken they ran for their lives, blindingly turning down lanes desperate to get away. Through the diminishing roar, the cries of people, separated from their loved ones and friends carried through the heavy, choking swirls of acrid smoke. One man who immediately before the explosion stood admiring the majesty of the cathedral with his wife, clawed at the heavy air of foaming debris. He wandered, stunned, calling his wife's name, his blood shot eyes streamed with tears which ran down his cheeks, smearing the thick layer of dust and blood covering his face and clinging to his clothes. She had been smashed by a section of the cathedral wall, her body carried away as it hurtled through the air taking all before it. His cries joined an ever growing chorus from dazed survivors, roaming around the mountainous pile of rubble.

A frantic knock on the office door and Sebastian was joined by his personal secretary, startled by the dramatic entrance he looked up from his paperwork with an angry frown.

'What?' Sebastian said gruffly, then regretting it as he saw the expression on her face.

'C-Canterbury sir' the secretary stammered out.

'Sorry?'

'Canterbury Cathedral has been blown up sir! The loss of life is expected to be high, the building has completely collapsed!'

Sebastian stared bewildered 'My God!' he whispered under his breath.

Before the words had left his mouth the phone on his desk rang. The Ambassador had now also been informed, and requested their immediate audience.

Sebastian and his secretary marched down the corridor, elaborately decorated with highly ornate frescos, no words were exchanged, both deep in thought. As they entered his make shift office, they were greeted by a sombre looking man, the weight of events plainly evident.

'Take a seat. The news I have received from London and the various news agencies this morning is extremely grave. At approximately 10.15 a huge bomb was detonated inside Canterbury Cathedral which has resulted in, according to the early reports, a complete collapse of the building. There would appear to be many casualties. At this moment in time no one has been pulled alive from the rubble. There are also many casualties outside of the cathedral as well. As you can imagine news is being received every minute, and the picture is extremely confused. But it would be fair to say it is a scene of complete devastation.'

'Sir this is just…' Sebastian struggled to find the words.

'I know Sebastian,' the Ambassador felt his envoy's incredulity. 'I believe we would not be a million miles away from suggesting this atrocity is the work of the same group which carried out the murder of Pope Steven here last week. But, we have to be careful before jumping to assumptions and conclusions.'

'Sir, this attack on the cathedral was obviously an attack

upon the Archbishop....albeit we are talking about the same faction who attacked the Pontiff. I am not sure about yourself, but when we received the details of the note found with the body I assumed any future target would have been elsewhere. Certainly not the Archbishop of Canterbury!'

'Quite right' replied the Ambassador 'we are, frighteningly, dealing with a terror group which has no compunction in dealing out horrific attacks at targets that frankly we have not been prepared for. The murder of the Pope was a surprise, there were no warnings or suspicions. This attack has once again caught us off guard. I have been asked to compile a profile of the Pope's speeches. The message he has been sending out to the world, we need to establish if there is any comparison with any issues the Archbishop of Canterbury may have brought up. There has to be a link! Sebastian I want you to go back to the beginning of Pope Steven's office in the Vatican, study his speeches, his documents, try and find anything which could be considered controversial. The nuncio has promised me his full support.'

Sebastian interrupted 'this may provide us with a template that can be used against agendas set by other religious leaders. We then may be able to predict a link, and ultimately who the next target may be.'

The Ambassador looked stern and thoughtful, 'whilst it is going to be a difficult, complex task, I do not have to remind you time may well be a luxury we cannot afford. We have to try and ascertain what the hidden agendas are which have brought about these heinous crimes.'

'Come on Cam, quick!' Josh beckoned as they walked

down to the wood next to Crawford Lake. The dusk light ebbed away as the sun sunk lower to the horizon. Crawford Lake rippled as the wind freshened from the north east. Grey wisps of cloud lined with red sailed across the sky.

'How much further Josh? It's going to be dark soon, and I have some work to finish before tomorrow.'

Josh carried on marching. 'It's down by the edge of the wood, if we don't hurry we might be too late.'

'Too late for what?' asked Cameron.

'You'll see.'

The outline of the individual trees started to lose their defined lines and shape as the sinking sun turned them into a congealed block of black. The boys had to begin treading with slower, purposeful steps as the trail began to hide the protruding roots and brambles.

'Josh did you bring the torch?'

'Of course I did' replied Josh, his voice not betraying what he thought of the fact Cameron had to ask. 'The batteries are a little low though, so I will use it when we get a bit nearer.'

They continued to tentatively step towards the wood, Josh stepped off of the track and turned on the torch and searched, probing the beam around the long grass.

'Here Cam, over here!'

On the edge of the trail, right on the boundary of the wood Cameron peered over Josh's shoulder. In a bowl of flattened grass, a small rabbit lay like a statue, the only sign of life was the rabbit's rapidly beating chest as it rose and fell with fast shallow breaths.

'Here it is' Josh knelt down gently, Cameron bent further over steadying himself on Josh's shoulder. 'It must be hurt Cam, otherwise it would have bolted the first time I found it. Maybe it has injured one of it's back legs, and it can't run away.'

'What are you going to do with it then?' asked Cameron brusquely.

Josh craned his neck around, 'what do you mean? We need to help it. We can take it back to the dormitory, see what is going on.'

Josh slowly reached out his hand towards the rabbit's head, still it did not move, continuing to breath rapidly. The noise of it's panting becoming louder as the three of them were finally gripped by the dark as the setting sun finally sank below the horizon. Josh's finger tips touched the rabbit's ears, they were soft and cold, laying flat back on it's head. Josh very gently moved his fingers down it's neck starting to feel some warmth through the fur.

'I wish I had brought a box.'

'A box! Josh this rabbit is half dead, what do you think you are going to be able to do. If it has got a broken leg or something it will need a vet.'

'That's ok, we can take it to nurse Isobel and she can help us. Come on Cam we can't just leave it here.'

'Out of the way Josh let me have a look.'

The two boys fumbled around each other careful not to trip over in the dark. Josh moved back as he saw Cameron bend over to look at the rabbit. He shivered, the wind finding a way down behind his coat. Josh was distracted by the hoot of an owl deep within the wood, suddenly he felt a dull thump on the ground, lifting the torch he lit up Cameron's face.

'Cameron? What did you do? What was that thump?' Josh tried to get past Cameron who just stood his ground.

'Cam what did you do?' Josh's voice quivered as he realised what the thud meant.

'It was the kindest thing to do' said Cameron coldly.

'Kind? What to kill her, we didn't even know what was wrong, we could have made her better!' Josh shouted.

'Behave Josh, it was for the best. It was a wounded animal it needed to be put down.'

Cameron went to pass Josh to return back to the dormitory. Josh didn't move. A rage built up inside him, he lifted his hand which held the torch and he swung his fist catching Cameron square in the middle of his chest. Cameron shocked by the blow, not expecting his smaller friend to hit him, stumbled backwards. He lost his balance and fell onto his bottom with a jar sending a painful sensation throughout his spine. Josh stepped over Cameron.

'I don't know what is wrong with you lately, but I should put you down!' said Josh through gritted teeth. He lifted his hand up again but stopped himself from hitting Cameron. A tear fell down his cheek, he turned and ran back up the trail to the school.

Jetrel sniggered, with a powerful swish of his wings he hovered above Cameron. He sensed the cold despair ebb throughout Cameron, The Fallen's patience was beginning to be rewarded. He twisted and swooped away low over the lake disappearing into the blackness.

Cameron brushed himself down, rubbed the sore point on his chest where Josh had hit him. Felt for the sore point at the base of his spine. He shouted after him, and as best he could ran up the trail. Cameron peered up ahead, he could not make out Josh in the thick, enveloping blackness but could see a small light dancing back and forth.

'Josh! Josh! Wait up!'

Malach was confused. The Fallen were not known for their hospitality. If I am within the realm of The Fallen why would they think I am a threat? That angel appeared to have enough power to wipe out the light from within me with one flap of his wing, let alone the swift justice I would receive from the legions of the Sable Core, should I be reaping death and destruction throughout the dark city. Still the reality of never knowing of another angel to be taken, and then released or lived to tell the tale about it was a concern. This might be a ploy. Malach laughed out loud. What ploy you fool? What could The Fallen ever gain out of a protector, let alone a protector who has failed in his duty with his first ever entity.

Malach wandered up and down the room, as far as his shackles would allow. Of course, what a better way to satisfy their sense of cruelty. A quick death, no. A friendly welcome, leading down a path of false security then wheeled out to the court of The Fallen and cast into the Fires of the Damned. Malach would not allow them to see the shock on his face when this happened, he decided he would not be taken in by their deceit. He would stay strong, not show any chink of weakness. When he was to die, he would die with the little honour that he had left. The air swirled within the wall, Samsaweel appeared.

'Ah Malach.'

'What do you want Samsaweel?' Malach said with contempt. He instantly saw the difference in comparison to his last visitor.

'Malach come, the time for hostility has gone. I'm not here to gloat. No, I am here to see how you are. As you can see the opportunity for escape does not exist. You have no where to go so why not do yourself a favour, and see how we can help you.'

'You help me? And why would you want to do that?'

Samsaweel paused. He knew he had to choose his words wisely, the protector must not see through the veil of deception.

'Look, we are not the murderous choir of angels who indulge ourselves within a realm of anarchy. We are the persecuted, we seek only to protect ourselves from the great deceiver.'

'The great deceiver?'

'Yes' Samsaweel replied intently. 'We would like you to see how this deceit has coloured the image of us; it would be an opportunity for you, if you so wish, to see the other side of the story. The facts as you within the kingdom of light never get to see, or to put it in a more finer way, what the Aleph would not allow you to see.'

'Never!' Malach snapped 'I know your game Samsaweel, you take me for a fool at your peril.'

Samsaweel laughed mockingly.

'Take note of your predicament protector, peril? Well I'm sure when Lucifer returns to you, he will let you have some understanding of the word you use so inappropriately.'

'Lucifer!' Malach said under his breath, the cold realisation hit home.

Cameron continued to stumble and grope his way back up to the school. He pushed open the heavy door and saw Josh running up the large staircase.

'Josh, come on, you are being really unreasonable!'

Josh stopped half way up, Cameron stood in the grand hallway. Marbled busts of past headmasters lined the edges of the walls, the marble floor was slippery under his trainers which were damp from the dewy grass. Josh turned, Cameron could see that his eyes were blood shot, a silvery trail running from his nose.

'Unreasonable, me!' Josh's voice quivered. 'You just killed that rabbit in cold blood. We could have saved it, or at least tried. I don't know what is going on Cam, and to be honest I don't want to know.' He rubbed his nose with the length of his forearm. 'I'm not sure I want to know you anymore' Josh's voice tailed off as he softly sobbed.

'Josh, what I did was the kindest thing. That rabbit wouldn't have survived. If you hadn't found it in the first place it would have ended up being eaten by a fox. Survival of the fittest.'

'What tosh!' interrupted Josh. 'Survival of the fittest? A little while ago Cameron you would have run back, got something to carry it with and we would have been hiding it in our lockers. But you just stamped on it! Murder!'

Josh ran up the stairs leaving Cameron alone, silence began to crowd him from all sides.

He shook his head, knowing what his friend was saying was right. But times change, people change. Why should he worry about a rabbit when there were people dying for no real reason as far as he could understand. He was on his own, surviving!

Chapter Five

Michael walked the city walls, Gabriel had joined him noticing a hint of sullenness. The news of the slaying of another Bridge-Maker along with hundreds of innocents had stunned the angel councils. The scrolls had not prepared the various councils of the possibility that a second Bridge-Maker would be targeted. Protectors at an alarming rate were being attacked the light from them extinguished; one protector had disappeared altogether without a trace of his fate or whereabouts. The hum of serenity surrounding the kingdom belied the greying atmosphere growing within man's kingdom.

'Michael?'

'Can you feel it Gabriel? We have lost our focus, and now we are going to see the consequences of our complacency. The assumption The Fallen are at the heart of the attacks on the Bridge Makers, would not be misplaced. My concern is why we have been blind to these events. A shadowed hand is gaining a firm grip on the minds and actions of man, you can feel we are at the lowest point of our influence. These killings will only serve the deeper cause of the dark.'

The two archangels continued to stroll slowly around the inner third wall of the city, banners fluttering gently in the breeze.

'Michael has it not always been that way? The Fallen have always sought to seek the mind of man for their own ends.'

Michael acknowledged Gabriel's question with a slight nod.

'Yes but I believe we are once again feeling the pressures of a new uprising. Potentially far more serious than anything we have seen before Gabriel. At present we are unknowing of their path to bring us to our knees.'

'The Fallen have always had their daemons accompany leaders of nations and at times the messengers of the light,' replied Gabriel. 'Hand in hand, they have been responsible for the conundrum of words laid upon on the people they are supposed to serve, whilst carrying out actions which only profit themselves and individuals who support them. This, ultimately, benefit's the cause of Lucifer and his followers. Always has.'

Gabriel acknowledged the salute of a guard as they passed, Michael did not noticed him.

Michael paused, turned to look out towards the two peaks, he placed his hands on the walls appearing to rest his body from the weight of foreboding pressing down on his shoulders.

'What lessons has man learnt from history? The paradox Gabriel, is man's inability to learn from the events of history, although he has the ability to send his peers to the moon, to invent and re-invent the wheel.'

'Michael, The Fallen's warriors create the barrier to man's desire to seek reconciliation,' said Gabriel 'to shake hands and put aside differences, to learn from history's events. During the 2nd Battle of Zo-Har, entities of the Juda faith looked skyward, all around them within the confines of their new world, a world surrounded by wire fencing, surrounded by the stench of death and disease, surrounded by human suffering on a level that would have been incomprehensible to them a few years before; before The Fallen had mobilised in their latest war against the Aleph. Through the dark ash leaden clouds rising continuously skywards, we could hear whispered words softly mingled with the souls of those passing beyond the two peaks, "God has abandoned us!" Michael, the Battle of Zo-Har almost brought the Enlightened to their knees, The Fallen struck powerfully at the very core of man's being, they massed at the walls of our city.' Gabriel said gesturing his arm at the vast expanse of land in front of the walls. 'The Fallen stretched our resources to the point where we could not be there for all, our protectors were decimated. The Fallen managed to corrupt leaders and intervene into the logic of those who would have opposed them, we never abandoned anyone.'

Michael did not reply, he caught site of a cavalry unit, far below going through the Gate of Arabah, out to patrol the border at the far side of the snow peaked mountains. Their gold armour shimmered, the banners at the top of the spears danced, giving the impression the falcon emblems were in flight around their heads. The unicorns walked in twos, heads lolloped sniffing the air, their riders sat upright, alert, moving in unison with the unicorn's majestic gait.

'The Battle of Zo-Har Gabriel, taught us to never underestimate the dark angels, if we ever did in the first place.' Michael's wings flickered, as he tugged at the bottom of his cloak, sweeping it across his shoulder. 'Gabriel, I will be going to The Collective, I fear we may have a traitor within these walls.'

Gabriel stared at him mulling through the implications of Michael's words.

'A traitor? Never!'

'It has to be the explanation as to why we have not been prepared for the slaying of the Bridge Makers.'

'Michael we are not always privy to the movements of The Fallen and where they will strike next' replied Gabriel.

Michael narrowed his eyes, thoughtful, looking after the cavalry scouts disappearing into the distance.

'I know, but an event which causes many entities too pass through the peaks is not something we would not be totally unprepared for. Yes, if The Fallen find a way of capitalising on it we may be caught off guard. Gabriel there are events that do not make sense. I do not have all the answers, any answers, just a sense!'

Samsaweel stood nervously as Lucifer toyed with the black crystal ball, inside it clouds swirled around.

'My prince, as ordered the light has been taken from another entity, the body will be discovered on the outskirts of the city of Canterbury. Everything is going to plan, further pawns sacrificed in the pursuit of chaos and your ultimate victory.'

Lucifer glared deeply into the ball. 'The boy has allowed the daemon to see some of the vision, how much?'

'Not enough my prince,' Samsaweel quickly interjected before Lucifer could reply 'but he is succumbing to us far quicker than we could have imagined. Of course with his protector safely occupied. We are now free to…..'

'We!' growled Lucifer. He glared down at the archangel and stood, his wings spread wide, casting a deep shadow over the dais, a sure sign Lucifer was not pleased.

Samsaweel instinctively bowed his head.

'Archangel, this boy does not need his protector around

him to resist us. He has an insight not seen in any entity since the cursed Aquinas! You underestimate this entity's resolve at great personal risk.'

Samsaweel felt a tightening around his neck, his throat crushed inwards. He fell to his knees, his body paralysed in an aura of evil. His vision began to blur, the great hall began to spin, gaining greater speed as the pressure around his neck tightened. Lucifer returned his stare back to the clouded orb. The pressure around Samsaweel's neck eased, the archangel slumped to the floor filling the great hall with huge gasps for air. His mind throbbed as the energy within him flowed back in a great rush.

Lucifer continued, unconcerned at the archangel's state. 'If the entity manages to seek the answers in his vision before we can, then all may be lost. It is a result that will have intolerable rewards for many including yourself. Am I understood archangel?'

Samsaweel rubbed his neck 'Yes my Lord.'

'Now go, I have an appointment with our guest.'

Cameron re-read the letter he had just finished, written on a free page deep inside his diary. Placed there in a subconscious attempt to keep it a secret to any would be readers, apart from the recipient.

> Mum,
> I have done something really bad. I have done something you would be very upset at, and I have really upset Josh. He hasn't spoken to me for a long time and I miss him. In a different way to missing you, but I wish he would accept my apology. I understand why he is so angry with me, but I just

wanted to see if I was right about God not doing anything to help people. I know you would be very angry with me too, but I think you out of everyone must understand why. I don't know what came over me, it was something that I didn't think about. if I could I would take it back.

How can I make Josh see it was a really big mistake?

Wish you were here mum X

The dinner bell rang and Cameron closed his diary. He placed it safely away in the bottom of his trunk which was stored away in his cupboard. Turning his bedside light off he made his way to the dining room, within the school corridors the bell's clank was just bearable, merging into the background as pupils spilled out of the classes, dormitories and common rooms. He was jostled by the stampede of boys eager to relieve their starvation brought on by the four hour gap since breakfast. Cameron was now feeling ever more lonely and isolated as the days passed since the incident with the rabbit. Josh had completely ignored him, choosing to sit on different tables in class, avoiding the common room when Cameron was there and even sitting at later meal sittings. Something Josh would never had contemplated in the past. Cameron thus far had not attempted to approach his friend, a few attempts of reconciliation had been sternly pushed away; he knew he had deeply wounded him, an upset he may never be forgiven for.

Jetrel sat on a large beam in the vaulted ceiling of the school dining room. Below him a raucous bustle of activity played out, as pupils came and went. Each sitting ushered in by the teachers as quickly and with as much control as was feasible when dealing with hundreds of ravenous boys with appetites resembling a plague of locust. Cameron placed a mountainous mass of baked beans all over his mash and sausages, then pushed his tray over to the puddings, opting for a small slice of Bakewell Tart; a sensible decision he thought as he had a double lesson of sports afterwards.

Cameron looked for a space at any of the dining tables, noting the only space available was opposite Josh. He sighed and with a shrug of his shoulders made for the chair. Cameron set his tray down on the table, Josh didn't look up. Cameron began to eat his meal through an uneasy quiet.

'Josh?'

'I have nothing to say to you!' Josh replied.

'Look I don't blame you for being upset with me. I'm sorry Josh, I don't know what came over me,' Cameron forked his beans through the mash tumbling it over until it became an orange goo. Josh didn't reply and continued to eat his meal.

'Josh please!'

'You tell me why I should forgive you? Why should I bother to talk to you?' Josh snapped.

'Because you're my friend. Because I haven't got anyone else. What I did was wrong, and if I could go back down to the wood and take back what I did Josh I would, but I can't. I have been far angrier with myself than you could ever be with me. Please Josh forgive me.'

Josh gently shook his head, and placed a large spoonful of Jam Roly Poly and Custard in his mouth, a small globule of custard caught the end of his mouth and sat precariously on the corner of his lip.

'I don't know what is happening with you Cam, but you have changed. Your mood changes, I don't know what you are going to be like when you wake up any more. One morning you seem to be happy, the next you won't talk unless you want something. What about Stuart?'

'What about Stuart?' Cameron asked

'In fencing last week, you attacked him so hard, your sword went underneath his mask and you flipped it off of his head cutting his chin. He said you looked like a madman!'

'I wanted to make the nationals, I had to win to ensure I would get into the team' Cameron explained coyly.

'Cam, Stuart has never beaten you, you were up in the competition and could have lost loads of points and still gone through, I saw you.' Josh scraped his bowl clean with the spoon, and took a gulp of squash swishing it around his mouth. 'You haven't done any of your project homework lately, you just watch television and read those books you got out of the library.'

Jetrel joined the boys and sat on the edge of the table opposite, his arms folded. The edge of his black cloak lay over a boy's plate of spaghetti bolognaise, the boy's fork twisted the spaghetti around creating an ever growing ball of pasta.

'What are all those books anyway?' Josh asked

'Nothing much' replied Cameron dismissively, which wasn't lost on Josh.

'Nothing much? During free time you are normally out and about, but now you spend most of it in the dormitory reading or in the common room watching the news.'

'I am just keeping up with some of the things that are

going on in the world that's all. My father has always said everyone should be aware of what is going on around them rather than just looking at the bubble that reaches the tip of their nose. Have you seen the stuff that has gone on down in Canterbury?'

Josh sat upright, an attempt to look as if he had some knowledge of it, until he had to open his mouth and the truth came out, 'Erm…..yes a little bit.'

'A little bit Josh! The Archbishop of Canterbury and hundreds of other people were blown up, the cathedral collapsed. This was after the Pope was shot. Don't you think it is something we should all be watching?'

'Well yes, but what has it got to do with me?' Josh took another large sip of squash, and stifled a choky cough. 'I can't do anything about it, can I?'

Cameron paused, Josh's common sense attitude stifled him. He knew Josh was absolutely right, what could he do about it. What could I do about it come to that? Cameron thought. If the Archbishop and the Pope were not able to stop what had happened then Josh is right. But surely that is the whole point, if the only person who could have done something about it is God, then why didn't he? Why would he let someone do that?

'No you couldn't do anything about it, but don't you see the problem? Why would God let it happen? He could have done something about it.'

Josh frowned.

'I mean, my mum, she was a good person and he let her die as well. If all these people are good and pray, then why does he let them die and be killed?'

Josh looked puzzled, all the questions Cameron fired at him churning around in his head. He rubbed his forehead.

'That's why....' Cameron paused, he looked around him and saw a lot of his fellow pupils had finished their meals and had left the dining hall to go to the common rooms or outside to play football. 'That's why I killed the rabbit!'

'What?' Josh said puzzled.

'Well, why would God let me kill a defenceless rabbit who could not defend itself; it just came to me in a flash, I didn't plan it or nothing, honest. But at that moment in time I thought if God was watching over us all and looking after us, which includes so we are told all the creatures as well. Then....'

'Then you thought you would see if God would stop you or punish you in some way for doing it' Josh's frown became even more pronounced.

'Well...erm....yeah.'

Josh puffed his cheeks out and transferred the bulge from one cheek to the other, then expelled the air through tightened lips making a loud squishing noise.

Jetrel stretched his wings in a satisfied arrogance, 'very well said!' he remarked. A large boy carrying his empty plates on a tray walked through his wing, Jetrel tutted 'why don't you look where you are going!' The boy carried on, placing his tray in the rack and left the room.

Cameron and Josh sat back in their chairs, Josh scraped his fork around his plate making swirly patterns in the gravy. Cameron turned to face Jetrel he looked through him but was sure he could see the flicker of air as a boy in the sixth form passed by. He looked back at his friend across the table, he felt a lot better he was able to talk to him. He hoped this constituted an acceptance of his apology.

'I keep seeing things Josh, well.....what I mean is that I

think I keep seeing things.'

Josh stopped playing with the cutlery and put his fork down. He did not reply but Cameron could see from his curious expression he wanted to hear more.

Jetrel also interested in hearing what Cameron meant, stood up and walked around to the empty chair next to Josh, he sat down and lent on the table.

'Mainly at night, I see an outline of a person, but I don't feel it is a person.'

'What is it then?' Josh asked.

'Well I'm not sure, I could be wrong or it could be the light playing tricks but sometimes I think I can see a wing.'

'What just a wing…what about the person?'

Cameron sighed. 'No Josh, not just a wing! I mean I see an outline of a person, and then what I think looks like a wing behind them.'

'It is probably the shadows Cam, that dormitory gives me the willies at night.'

'Yeah I know but you know the pressure thing I told you about a little while ago, well I feel it all the time now. It use to be every now and then, and I would think I heard things like voices. But would put it down to something else, well lately it has been with me all the time.'

The dining hall was now empty, apart from the dining staff banging the plates and cutlery as they collected them from the racks, talking and laughing loudly as they cleared up. One lady was unceremoniously pushing the chairs under the tables.

'The dreams I have still happen, that's what the books are about.'

'What a book about dreams?'

'No' said Cameron, 'I am trying to see if I can see any

pictures which are the same as the images I dream about. An old man, wearing a tabard, like our house ones.'

Josh frowned again.

'Or similar anyway.' Cameron quickly added before Josh could interject with "what he is wearing a green slip with the face of Nelson on it?" 'He is in an old room and reading a very large book and writing, he is always writing.'

'What is he writing about?' asked Josh.

'I don't know, I cant see. But it seems to get a little bit closer all the time, maybe one night I will actually get to see what he is writing.'

Cameron and Josh were interrupted by a lady standing at the edge of their table, 'have you boys finished with those?' she said pointing at the empty plates.

'Yes we have thanks' replied Josh, he placed his hand on his stomach and rubbed appreciatively thinking to himself supper seemed along way away.

'Well I had better take them then since you two boys seem routed to the spot' she grabbed the trays and left.

'Shall we go outside?' asked Cameron hoping Josh would say yes and not turn him away.

'Yeah, come on' replied Josh.

Jetrel knew Cameron's conversation with Josh contained far reaching implications, not only the dream and visions he had been warned about by Samsaweel, but the possibility the boy may be able to see through the angelic partition. Jetrel became surrounded with strange feelings of insecurities, he now felt very exposed. He knew that to leave the boy and report to Samsaweel would not sit well with the archangel, he had been ordered to stay with the entity at all costs. He was now alone in the dining hall, apart from the lady wiping the tables down with a cloth. Jetrel considered the possibility of punishment but decided this information was important, information Samsaweel would want to know. A powerful flick of his wings and Jetrel soared through the ceiling of the dining hall.

Chapter Six

As his chains would allow Malach paced, becoming more frustrated with every passing moment. The confines of his small room, his cell, echoed his cries straight back at him. What is happening to Cameron? He clinched his fists. Does the angel kingdom realise that I am a prisoner of The Fallen? If so, what are they doing about it? Malach sighed with a deep resignation. What could they do about it?

The protector had become fatigued with his constant thinking, he wished for a moment when he could feel some inner peace. The room was devoid of all other noise, it's silence overwhelming, his thoughts thunderous. You don't deserve any inner peace! You have failed yourself, the Aleph and more importantly your entity! Malach focused on a small blemish on the wall, directing his thoughts away from his torment.

'There isn't any need to reproach yourself protector!'

Malach twisted around sharply. Before him stood Lucifer.

'Lucifer' Malach whispered under his breath.

'Yes, the very same' replied the dark prince.

Malach as he did the first time, stood in awe of his magnificence. The stories he had heard did not do this angel justice, he pondered. The protector pulled his shoulders back, trying to portray an air of nonchalance, he would not allow Lucifer to see he had any affect on him. Lucifer naturally saw straight through the pointless gesture.

'You do yourself an injustice. You have let no one down. If anything it is you who have been let down Malach.'

Malach shuddered as Lucifer spoke his name.

'I have been let down? By whom?' he asked.

Lucifer smiled, the dark prince had managed to engage the protector into conversation, a door had opened, an opening he would exploit.

'Do you need to ask? You know the answers Malach. You just need to open yourself up to the truth, you have been fed a maelstrom of deceit. Deceit that, given the opportunity we can put right.'

'I have been fed nothing of the sort!' Malach replied.

'I don't expect you to believe me protector, why would you just take my word for it. I am prepared to show you.'

Lucifer waved his hand, the air parted and Malach was enveloped in a dusty heat. The image surrounded him, as it became clearer they now stood in the middle of a dry Indian mud road filled with men on motor scooters, oxen pulling carts and street urchins carrying containers of water on their heads. To the side of the road Malach could see a shabby brick temple ornate with painted images of a God. Men dressed in well worn, threadbare clothes hung loosely; the skin of their hands and face stained with a deep rust red, caused by their cutting tools which sent asphyxiating clouds of miniscule metal shards into the air, walked amongst the traffic and smog, on their way home after a long shift at the ship breaking yard. Each one stopped at the temple, lit a candle and said a quick prayer to their God, thanking him for protecting them through their day. Behind them through the gates of the shipyard they had left six of their colleagues dead; a higher than average toll for a days work. The men returned to their homes, huts devoid of any running water, any sanitation, a rickety wooden bed. For some, maybe the luxury of having a worn rug on the floor. Before they eat they gathered down at the river and attempted to wash off the soil of their days graft. Their meagre wages just enough to purchase a bowl of rice. Once eaten, they again prayed to their God before going to their beds, to rest weary, broken, hungry bodies. Ready for the same cycle of life the following day.

'Why are you showing me this?' Malach asked.

'Where is their God? Where is the Aleph Malach?'

Malach did not answer, unsure Lucifer was luring him down into a trap.

'Well protector? These entities show reverence, and trust unto him with all their being. They believe he defines their destiny. Yet what reward is there for this devotion. Hunger! Disease! Hopelessness!' Lucifer dropped his hand, the vision faded, and Malach was once again trapped by the walls of his cell. 'Funny isn't it protector. All the things associated with the so-called Fallen.'

Malach shifted his gaze to the floor, he felt the air pulse in front of him, Lucifer disappeared from the room.

The unicorns preferred the lush feel of the grass, rather than the hard surface of the marbled road which ran parallel to the River Nephesh. Behind the cavalry unit the Gate of Arabah receded into the distance. As they trotted along the river bank, the pebbly river bed could be easily seen through the crystal clear water. A fish broke the surface, jumping completely out of the water, it's arched flight ended with a soft splash then darting away leaving a trail of bubbles behind it. The river emanated from the Sea of Souls. It ran through the city, appearing in the pastures of the angel realm, growing larger and travelled throughout the kingdom, a source of life and attachment to the city itself. Tributaries branched off, rapids became small waterfalls falling into gentle lakes. A powerful branch of the river cut straight through the middle of The Forest of Wandering Spirits, disappeared between the two peaks, becoming the awesome waterfall which fell between the two enormous angel wings of the conduit.

The angel troopers of the cavalry unit looked around them across the plains of the kingdom. Ahead of them in the distance the forest hid the base of the two peaks which appeared to rise out of the very forest itself. The snow tipped mountains even though far in the distance commanded the horizon. The white plumes from their helmets fluttered behind them, the white falcon insignia on their cloaks flew in unison with the falcon on their banners. The troopers trotted across a bridge spanning a tributary, one of many fingering their way across the pastures, set free by the great River Nephesh.

The commander of the troop heard some of his troops talking about the rumours spreading rapidly within the kingdom regarding the assassinations of the Bridge Makers, he let the small talk continue. Zahabriel had heard his fellow officers talking about the killings and the possible meanings behind them; he was always struck by the way angels accompanied man in their ability to bring a rumour to life and let it runaway like a feather travelling down the falls of the River Nephesh. He was an experienced officer, rumour and whispers were not to be tolerated, they were the play thing of the foolish. Decisions based on hard facts had given him a reputation amongst his troops of a leader who never panicked, a commander who dealt with issues in a clear and balanced manner.

Zahabriel looked into the distance, he could now see where the marbled road entered the forest, in the far distance he could just begin to make out the roar of the falls.

'Quiet there!' he shouted, the troops instantly responded to his command. The Forest of Wandering Spirits was the boundary of their patrol, it was the stepping stone to the conduit of man's world, which was also the gate through which angel or beast entered the angel kingdom. As they entered the forest, the thick canopy stemmed the bright light of the Aleph. Zahabriel took a brief moment to adjust to the shade, the noise of the plains and the song of the River Nephesh became muffled, disappearing completely as they ventured deeper into the trees. The forest held an ungainly hush about it.

Zahabriel looked to his left sharply as a shadow darted between the trees. Looking up towards the chinks of light spearing through the tree tops, his senses grasped for the cause of the silence that now prevailed.

'Sir?'

'I know' replied Zahabriel to the nervous trooper, with a glance back noticing the rest of the angels apprehensively looking all around them. A unicorn in the middle of the troop became jumpy, it's rider tightened his grip on the reins, reassuring the unicorn with a slap on it's neck.

'Steady there!' Zahabriel snapped. 'Keep a sharp eye, troopers to the left concentrate your field of view to your left, troopers to the right concentrate your field of view to the right. Report what you actually see, not what you think you see!'

Zahabriel kept the twenty nine troopers moving through the forest, the silent foreboding grew stronger the deeper they went. The soft rustle of the leaves boomed around them.

'Sir, to the right!' a trooper cried out pointing into the dense tree line.

Zahabriel craned his neck round to look, standing in the stirrups, but saw nothing.

'What was it trooper, what did you see?'

'Erm…..I'm not sure sir' the trooper suddenly questioned himself, did he see something or was it his imagination. 'It was a shadow sir, a movement just over there where the woodland clears a fraction. But I could not make out what the movement was exactly.'

'Troop!' Zahabriel shouted 'keep a sharp eye, at the canter we will make for the clearing ahead' he lifted his banner into the air, and with a sharp jerk downwards the cavalry troop as one kicked into a canter.

The cavalry troop entered the clearing, it was bright as the canopy opened allowing a great shaft of light to enter.

'Atarah!' Zahabriel commanded.

The two columns parted. Each line then arched inwards creating a circle. The unicorns faced outwards, their troopers braced their spears with the shafts pointing over the heads of the unicorns, pointing slightly skyward ready to drop them if the circle was attacked. Their long shields unclipped, each angel braced them tight against their sides. The falcon crested shields and chest armour of the unicorns reflected the insignia outwards, Zahabriel was in the middle of the Atarah, his unicorn spinning on the spot, fifty eight shimmering spears and unicorn horns penetrated into the forest, the Atarah was complete, a protective crown.

Zahabriel clicked his tongue, dug his heels into Sapientia's belly. Pulling on the reins he settled her into a slow walk around the inner perimeter of the crown.

'Steady now' he said, 'report what you see, and only what you see.'

Zahabriel adjusted his helmet strap, tightening it pulling the cheek pieces closer to his face. He twisted the shaft of his spear rotating it in it's pommel.

'There sir!' a trooper called out, before he could bring his spear down to point in the direction, an arrow imbedded itself in his eye, travelling deep into his head. He tipped forward onto his unicorn's neck, slumped sideways and fell to the ground. The unicorn skipped backwards into the crown, just missing Zahabriel's unicorn.

'Close Atarah!' Zahabriel barked.

The gap closed, the troopers tensed, eyes searching desperately into the distance. Troopers began to call out all around the circle.

'Ok save your breath, keep shields up and be ready for a sudden attack' Zahabriel spoke in a calm voice. He knew only the foolish would charge head on into an intact Atarah. Slow attrition would be the most likely action, an opportunity to weaken the circle then once a gap was created, a frenzied charge.

Zahabriel heard the faint whisper of arrows flying from the tree line, 'Shields!' he cried.

Several arrows flew over the heads of the outer troops, narrowly missing Zahabriel, landing in the ground. A sickening cry from a unicorn pierced the air as an arrow bit deep into it's exposed thigh, the pain forced it's leg to buckle. Frantically it's rider pulled on the reins; the unicorn tried to put weight through the leg, as it did it let out a piercing whinny and stumbled sideways. The angel trooper was thrown, his spear falling from his grip. The breath knocked out of him, he took a moment to gain his senses. He crouched, feeling woefully exposed the trooper held his shield in front of him, and fumbled to grasp the hilt of his sword, trying to pull it free from it's scabbard. Behind him he heard Zahabriel shout for the circle to close the gap over the whinnying of his mortally injured unicorn.

'Come on' beckoned Zahabriel to the exposed trooper 'shield up and tread backwards, when you get to us we will open the crown!'

The trooper nodded nervously. The cavalry commander could see the fear deep within his eyes. He began to step back slowly as he crouched behind his shield, the shield suddenly felt wholly inadequate for it's intended purpose of protection and the angel trooper tried to crouch even tighter.

'Shields!' Zahabriel cried out again. A volley of dark arrows flew from the trees once again. Two troopers who did not react quick enough paid for it with their lives, one of the troopers fell backwards over the rump of his unicorn landing in a heap of armour and cloak next to Zahabriel. He dug his heels into the soft underbelly of Sapientia and gripped the reins to stop her bucking. The gap closed again. He turned and stared down at the trooper who had been flung outside of the Atarah, now standing next to him adjusting his helmet. He had seen the opportunity and charged through the gaps before they closed. He stared up at his cavalry commander, noticing Zahabriel was now looking down at him, he snapped to attention. The unicorn who had lost her trooper in the first attack was still within the circle. Zahabriel ordered him to mount the unicorn and rejoin the Atarah. He saluted. The cavalry commander then saw his eyes glaze over, the trooper mouthed some words but the voice never left his mouth, an arrow had penetrated straight through his neck. The trooper's shield arm flopped to his side, the weight of his shield pulled him sharply sideways. He was dead before he hit the ground.

War horns blasted throughout the forest.

'Damn!' mumbled Zahabriel under his breath. 'Deliver me from the lion's mouth, and my lowliness by the horns of unicorns.'

A crack of thunder startled Sebastian. Strange he thought thunder in March? He gazed out of his study window, the full moon was bright in a cloudless sky. He rubbed his eyes, and returned to the dark oak study table. A small lamp sent a dim glow over a pile of paperwork, he walked over to a large globe drinks cabinet in the corner of the room to pour himself another generous measure of port. Large book cabinets hung from the walls, containing his vast collection of antiquarian and first edition books.

Sebastian had been sent home by the Ambassador to see if he could gather any information on the attack on Canterbury Cathedral which would tie in with the assassination of Pope Steven. He had read through reams of Pope Steven's speeches given over the five years as the Catholic leader. Nothing within the words the pontiff had spoken betrayed any underlying reason for someone to be driven to kill him. Sebastian sat back in his tall leather chair, the killings of the two religious leaders had caused factions to point accusing fingers at each other. Small riots had broken out in various cities around the world. More worryingly in Sebastian's opinion was the targeting of religious groups by right wing parties eager to capitalise on any open door of turmoil. Jewish and Muslim businesses had been attacked, buildings burnt down with no care for the safety of the people that may have been inside. He glanced at the shadowy framed picture of his wife, Rebecca. It was a photograph he had taken of her, whilst on holiday when courting. He missed her desperately. From the moment he woke to the moment he fell asleep, she was with him. Rebecca's presence was always in the back of his mind, no matter what he was doing or thinking, she was there. Always there. At times the pain of his loneliness surrounded him in an oppressive cocoon, at times he had felt weak by remaining strong. In his private moments of weakness he would close his eyes and wish the world away, just to be able to be with her, just to speak to her. He would speak to Rebecca, ask her questions, even hear her voice from past remembered conversations. The hardest moments were when he could feel her embrace, the warmth and tenderness. Moments of true love which now flooded him with an inner pain, a shroud of hurt that with the passing of time became harder to deal with, rather than easier. He closed his eyes, immersing himself into the moment only to get angry at his weakness, angry for allowing his protective barrier to be penetrated.

'Sebastian?'

He had not heard Emily enter the study; he became embarrassed, hoping she had not seen his privates thoughts. She hadn't.

'Emily, are you ok?'

'Yes, I was just off to get a hot drink. The door was open and I saw a light on. Thought I heard thunder, must have been dreaming' she said.

'No, there was a clap of thunder. Only one, no rain or lightning though. Must be the spring winds coming early and driving out the winter cold.'

She could see Sebastian was tired, he rubbed his eyes wearily and toyed with some papers on his desk.

'You should get some sleep Sebastian, you arrived this morning and haven't stopped working. Would you like a hot drink?'

Sebastian thought for a moment. 'No thanks Emily. You are right I should get some sleep. I haven't spoke to Cam for a couple of days has he been ok? I presume he has been otherwise I would have heard.'

Emily drew her dressing gown tighter as the chill of the night made her shiver. 'Yes he is fine. He had a little falling out with Josh last week, did he say?'

Sebastian shook his head.

'It wasn't much apparently, something about a rabbit but he didn't elaborate, typical boys, best of friends now.'

Sebastian had his laugh stifled by a yawn.

Emily smiled, she could see all the paperwork on his desk, relating to the murders of the Pope and Archbishop, but she never questioned or talked about his work. Emily for the most part was actually never interested. Her role was to make sure Sebastian and Cameron were looked after, this was all she was concerned about.

'Your paperwork will still be there in the morning, or in a few hours time to be precise!' Emily said.

Sebastian knew by the tone of her voice and the expression on her face it would be futile to argue, anyway she was right he thought, which was not really a great position to base an argument on. He nodded and switched the lamp off. Another clap of thunder rumbled outside.

'Hold! Close the gaps when they appear!' Zahabriel shouted as loud as he could to make himself heard over the war horns of The Fallen. The cavalry commander knew to stay in the clearing would ultimately bring disaster, a slow death. To charge into the tree line and attempt to bring The Fallen to a clash of arms, would be folly. Where were they? How many were there? Isolated troopers surrounded would be cut down mercilessly. If The Fallen were prepared to stay in the shadows, Zahabriel decided the only option was to turn and run and hopefully live to fight another day. He came over to the side of the Atarah facing the trail back through the forest towards the city. The attacks seemed to be concentrated on three sides, the side of the Atarah facing the trail had suffered no casualties. Zahabriel knew the risks, to turn and show your back on the enemy could bring disaster; to stay would mean no less he decided.

'On my command, we will move towards the trail keeping the Atarah connected. Then in stages the Atarah will melt at the point of the trail. Ride as fast as you can back to the city. Do not stop whatever happens behind you!' As Zahabriel finished, another volley felled three troopers. 'Close up!' he shouted.

'Right, on my command. Move!'

The ever decreasing circle, moved as one down the trail. Luckily the Atarah had been formed within a short distance of the trail as they had entered the clearing. Zahabriel kept a watchful eye on the far tree line in case The Fallen seized the opportunity to attack. The first two angel troopers disappeared down the trail, the circle became a tight arc with each rider at it's edge, kicking his heels and driving the unicorns into the forest away from the clearing. Zahabriel kept facing the far tree line. As the last two riders kicked off, he pulled sharply on Sapientia's reins, she began to turn instantly responding to the command, out of the corner of his eye he suddenly saw the tree line ripple as The Sable Core surged into the clearing after them.

Zahabriel did not look back, he kicked his heels and surged his hands forward urging his unicorn to gallop faster. The cavalry of the Sable Core rode the winds of discontent, they spread their wings, and were pushed forward as the winds filled their feathers. The dark cavalry were accompanied by packs of wolves, jet black and fearless, they were swift appearing to fly themselves. Zahabriel could feel the air pressure build behind him as the Sable Core chased them down. Just behind him to his left and right he could see the wolves attempting to overtake them up the sides and cut the troopers off before the could get out of the forest.

'Ride! Ride!' he shouted.

One of the angel troopers fell as the Sable Cavalry fired another hopeful volley.

Zahabriel forced himself to keep looking forward as he passed the prostrate body, urging Sapientia to go even faster, he could feel her heaving chest underneath him. In the ever nearing distance he could now see a chink of brightness at the edge of the forest increase, it spurred him on. He started to draw level with the trooper in front of him, the trooper kept nervously glancing from left to right. In an instant a black flash dragged him clean from the saddle, a wolf gripped him by his throat smothering his screams.

Another wall of arrows fell around him as he left the

forest, the dazzling light of the plains temporarily blinded him, he closed his eyes tight then blinked furiously.

Feeling the pressure around him ease he took a quick look behind him and saw nothing followed. The Fallen had stopped their chase at the edge of the forest, where nine of his troopers remained.

Chapter Seven

Jetrel sat perched on the roof of the school, as he looked across towards the horizon, the full moon was high in the sky. Crawford Lake shimmered silver with reflection. Jetrel used the lake as a stepping stone in his mind, bouncing over several other silver plates dotted across the blackened landscape. The daemon tugged at the top of his cloak which had snagged on the tip of his wing, as it freed he stretched it as wide as he could. Always fidgeting.

Jetrel pondered over the words spoken by Cameron. Had the boy actually seen him or was it just the shadows that he saw? It wouldn't be the first time an entity had claimed to have seen angels and miracles, only for it to be dispelled by a rational explanation by the disbelievers of mankind. Jetrel had decided that to return to the dark city would be unwise. He would report it to the archangel the next time he was summoned, it would be easier to plead ignorance to the fact the boy 'thought' he saw him, rather than explaining why he had disobeyed a direct order. Jetrel flicked his wings out, and with a gentle flap he rose slowly from the school roof, with a subtle twist he vanished through the roof, towards the sleeping Cameron.

The old man scribbled frantically, the sharp edge of the feather scratching over the parchment... The dream continued as it did almost every night, Cameron's eyes were shut tight but his dream state caused his eyes to flicker rapidly. In his dream he was desperately seeking the large book the old man was reading from, or the written parchments.

*The old man dipped his feathered quill into the inkpot, the pot was almost dry and his ink stained fingers lifted it to drain the remnants of ink to one side, scraping the quill through the miniscule pool that remained. The old man scratched a few more words, placed the feather into its holder in the wooden table, and took the ink pot over to the window where a small metalled jug stood on the window sill. He opened the window a little wider and looked down onto a large square. The suns rays were warm on his cheeks and he closed his eyes breathing deeply through his nose. The edges of his paperwork lifted gently with the breeze entering through the window, the top page rustled. The writing on the top page was exceptionally neat, very straight lines on plain parchment, flowing letters, a small ink smudge in the top corner....*The dream was broken by a sudden intense flash of white light, Cameron below could now see a storm at sea, he rushed towards a ship far below.....*Waves crashed over the bow of the ship, high in the masts sailors fought to haul the sodden sails in. Under the quarterdeck, seeking futile shelter, a knight wrapped in his cape, frantically tried to keep his footing on the dancing deck. The ship rose dramatically to the top of a huge wave, it cross-bowed sickeningly; a cry lost in the wind came from a sailor falling from the main mast, he ploughed into the stormy seas, disappearing forever. The bow dropped then drove deep into another mountainous wave, the ship faltered. The knight was thrown violently across the deck, the case he held under his cape fell from his grip, and skidded across the treacherous deck, the knight frantically* *scrambled on all fours, trying to reach it. Another huge, heavy wave hit the bow of the ship pushing it deeper downwards, overwhelmed it slipped, with all hands, beneath the waves.*

Cameron woke and sat upright.

He had never seen the ship or knight in his dream before, he wondered sleepily what it meant, his thoughts returned to the old man, Cameron had recognised a few of the words not so decoratively written.

'Latin!' he said 'the words he was writing were Latin.'

He did not recognise the words in the large book from which the old man was working from, but at least now he had something to grasp. The library would have many books on Latin. Cameron cleared the sleep from the corners of his eyes. As the gritty sleepiness cleared, standing at the bottom of his bed, he saw the figure of a man, Cameron could see a bulge protruding from each of his shoulders. The man was tall, as tall as his dad Cameron thought. Jetrel looked behind him, no one was there, he realised Cameron was looking at him, he stood dead still. If he did not move the boy might think it was his imagination played upon by the dark of the night.

'Who are you?' Cameron asked calmly, surprised at himself for not feeling afraid. He felt a pressure although it was somehow unfamiliar. Maybe it was because it suddenly came across as a strong pulse as if he was standing right beside the skin of a giant bass drum being beaten rhythmically.

Jetrel's mind spun, the boy could see him. Should he reply and see if he could hear the spoken words of an angel? The voice of an angel was a force which could not be tolerated by man, a force so strong death was a possibility.

Jetrel had never been in the position of actually speaking to an entity but he knew the teachings of the angels stated their voices were too pure to be heard by man. Jetrel stepped back into the shadows, now was the time for Samsaweel to be told. Cameron blinked, the man had gone.

A shadow? Cameron thought no not this time. Cameron plumped up his pillow and laid back down. As soon as he could he would visit the library.

Jetrel stood before Samsaweel, the daemon had taken a big risk in coming back to the dark city, disobeying a direct order from the archangel could have serious consequences. But the boy did see him; surely it was something the archangel would want to know. Samsaweel sat at the table looking at the daemon, he knew Jetrel was nervous about being in front of him, Jetrel had taken a risk and Samsaweel did not feel inclined to put him at ease. Not yet anyway. The information Jetrel had given him about the boy, put together some pieces of the jigsaw he had been receiving from The Fallen council. Samsaweel was beginning to see that far from being special and part of Lucifer's plans to win the angelic war, the boy was potentially something exceptional.

'What I would like to know is how you think this information about the boy is something new to me?' Samsaweel said condescendingly, it would not do for the daemon to think this archangel was not privy to all the minutiae of the dark city, he thought.

Jetrel swallowed hard.

'I meant no disrespect. I thought long and hard before leaving the entity. But if....' Jetrel placed a lot on emphasis on the word if, '....the information I bring was an unknown development it's importance would have required me to report to you immediately. I did not mean to suggest, by being here, you were not already aware.' Jetrel fidgeted nervously.

'Yes, that may well be the case. But what will not do is for daemons to think!' Samsaweel did not want this information getting into the hands of others until he informed Lucifer himself, someone such as Dalkiel would cast the last feather on his wings into the fires of damnation for this news.

'Come with me. I want to show you something I think you might be very interested to see. Once finished, I want you to return to the entity, and this time do not leave him. I will come to you or summon you, has that order been understood Jetrel?'

Jetrel bowed and followed Samsaweel out of the room.

Jetrel looked the guard who stood outside the cell up and down. The daemon himself, was an angel who would have graced any unit within the Sable Core but he was impressed with the powerful appearance of this angel. The air swirled and Samsaweel stepped through into the room, Jetrel followed.

Malach shook his head as his visitors walked in. This he did not need or want.

'Malach, how are you? Thought I would bring along a friend' Samsaweel smirked.

'You know Samsaweel sarcasm suits you' Malach replied, he walked towards the two dark angels, his chains stemming his progress.

'Malach, as I have said. You are our guest, it is up to you how much of our hospitality you are willing to accept.'

Malach looked beyond Samsaweel recognising the angel behind him. Jetrel held his hand up, smiled as if butter would not melt upon it.

'Come to gloat?' Malach hissed.

Jetrel smiled and spread his hands, 'Gloat? No Malach that's not my style. Was just passing thought I would come and see how you were getting used to the old place. Not bad is it?' Jetrel looked around the room nodding appreciatively. 'The young boy...what is his name? Cameron that's it. He is doing absolutely fine as well. Yes, we are just inseparable these days.'

Malach thrust forward, his chains rattled as he almost stumbled.

'If I get the opportunity dark angel you will regret the hospitality you have sent me too, and if the boy is harmed or lead towards the chaos you represent. I will make it my oath to never rest until you are sent into damned purgatory!'

Jetrel shook his head dismissively.

'Such strong words! It is that rash rush of blood oh Enlightened one which has led you to be in the position to use such rhetoric,' Jetrel stepped closer gloatingly, 'and unable to back it up.'

Malach this time did stumble as he surged at Jetrel, he stopped himself falling completely to the floor, his hands supporting him. Samsaweel brought his foot up into Malach's unprotected ribcage, just hard enough to blast the air from his lungs but not hard enough to leave any marks. As Malach lifted himself off of the floor the two dark angels left through the swirl of air.

'As soon as the last trooper is through the gate close it!'

Michael turned away from the officer of the guard and looked into the distance at the Forest of Wandering Spirits, twenty one individual clouds rapidly approached the city, 'as soon as Zahabriel gets back I want to see him immediately!'

Michael strode away his cloak twirling after him.

'Yes sire' replied the officer. Michael disappeared along the rampart, the city buzzed with anxiety as the war horns of The Fallen echoed across the plains of the angel kingdom.

Zahabriel entered the large hall of the Archangel Council, the seven archangels were sat on the dais. The cavalry commander walked towards them, his helmet under his arm, his white uniform covered in a film of dust. Michael ready in his battle armour, the gold chest armour embossed with the symbol of the sun. Gold cleaves on his legs and arms.

'What happened?' Michael asked sternly.

Zahabriel reported, he was an experienced officer, there would be no over embellishment just the facts as they happened.

'Were you able to gauge the size of the force?'

'No sire. I only saw shadows to begin with, when we entered the clearing they picked their targets carefully staying out of sight. The only time I saw them was when I ordered the troop back into the forest, they then broke from the tree line. But I only saw a few of The Sable Cavalry and The Sable Wolves.'

Michael looked thoughtful.

'You only lost nine troopers, your casualties were light,' Zahabriel knew what the archangel was leading to, it was not a criticism of his skills of leadership.

'Yes sire. The Fallen concentrated their attack on three sides of the Atarah. For some reason they did not close around behind us, allowing us the opportunity to break for the city. The attacks were also very conservative, they picked their targets. There were a few hopeful volleys but I expected a lot worse.'

Michael walked from the dais, leaving his fellow councillors sitting on their thrones. He slowly paced around the fountain in the middle of the hall, and stood at the window. He looked out across the Sea of Souls, the Gates of Arabah were now shut, the war horns of The Fallen had stopped and the city had been called to arms. Far in the distance he gazed at the two peaks, a grey mist now shrouded the forest.

'Why would they allow you to escape? Maybe they have sent a skirmishing force across, hoping that you, we, think it is a larger force which now occupies the forest and beyond,' Michael pondered.

Michael turned as Remiel interrupted. 'It may have been a scouting party, in front of the main body. Our cavalry needed to be stopped. An opportunist attack.'

'Yes, that is feasible Remiel. But why would they allow the troop to escape? If it was a scouting party they would have made every effort to annihilate the troop before they had a chance to raise the alarm' replied Michael.

Sariel stood, 'maybe they did not intend for them to escape. Zahabriel, through fine command was able to strike through into the forest on the weakened side of the Atarah, which they were too slow to strengthen.'

Zahabriel did not outwardly seem to react to the praise, inside he thought it was inappropriately directed. His fine command had left nine of his angels back in the forest.

Michael returned to the dais, he turned and looked down at the cavalry commander, 'three possibilities. First, it is how Remiel has stated, a scouting core in front of the main body, who saw an opportunity to attack and did so; but failed in wiping out the troop before they had a chance to escape. Second, a skirmishing party has broken through the conduit. Opportunists who were insufficient in numbers to close the trap; allowing an opportunity for Zahabriel to retreat. Or thirdly....' Michael paused '...thirdly, they wanted the troop to escape!'

The three captains of the Sable Core, Beleth, Bernael and Ertrael stood at the edge of the forest, beyond the city walls they could hear the frantic preparations of a city in organised panic.

'Seems as if we have caused quite a stir!' Ertrael sneered. He removed his helmet and pushed his jet black hair away from his heavily pronounced forehead. His tiny, perfectly spherical eyes were set deep into his head, giving the impression his cheek bones were in a permanent swollen state.

'Do you think they are pleased to see us?' replied Bernael, the taller of the three captains, his slender physique belied the strength of the cavalry commander.

Beleth, a heavy set angel, who carried the scars of many battles with the Enlightened on his face, turned to his fellow officers. 'Well, let us return to the encampment and begin to make plans to show them how much we appreciate their hospitality.'

The three captains of The Sable Core laughed, and returned into the cover of the forest.

Chapter Eight

Lucifer stood over the crouched figure of the protector. Malach rested his chin on his arms which lay across the tops of his knees. Lucifer paced slowly, his hands clasped behind his back.

'Malach what would we gain from guiding the leaders of man to profit from their position? It would not serve our purpose to prosper in the divide inhabiting man's being. That is the deceit you are fed. Is it not the right of every man to live with the promise of a future, the promise hard work will bring reward. The reward for prayer and servitude is what exactly?'

Malach kept his gaze directly on the floor in front of him.

'As a protector Malach, you have walked amongst man. As yet, you are not experienced enough to have walked amongst all men, but that will come. You will see in many parts of his world, the leaders of man's religion live in splendour whilst their flock pray to their God for the right to eat and live without disease and despair.'

Malach looked up at the dark prince, who raised his eyebrows at him questioningly, then returned his gaze to the floor.

'Can this be right Malach? Would any God allow the channels of his word and glory to bask in riches and self proclaimed adulation. When the common man who worships and reveres, living to your Aleph's law is rewarded with……with gratitude maybe; a promise of eternal life for living a life of damnation! You cannot seriously believe our influence is guiding the hands of all the messengers of the Aleph. Man's churches are full of gold, jewelled trinkets, treasures which could support the people they serve. It is The Fallen who are accused of dividing the populous through wealth, politic and the spread of dissension.'

Lucifer stopped pacing. Malach looked up and met his gaze.

'A cloak of deceit spread by the Enlightened, a cover which suits their purpose.'

Lucifer left.

Malach placed his head on his arms and closed his eyes. What is Lucifer, the prince of The Fallen doing speaking to a lowly protector? he thought. Why am I still alive? What would The Fallen have to gain from keeping me here? Malach thought about the visit of Samsaweel and Jetrel, he was gripped with anger as he saw Cameron in the shadows of his mind. Jetrel's admission he was now accompanying the entity made the protector think about The Fallen's motives. The boy was visited by an archangel of The Fallen, why would an archangel waste his time seeking out weaknesses within an entity who had no influence within his immediate world? The boy before his mother's passing showed a willing to reach out towards the angelic partition, he then as expected has joined the majority of men and rejected the words of his protector. Jetrel is no archangel, they have obviously seen the boy is as any entity, ultimately, fashioned by his society. Left to be guided by a daemon. Malach with a groan stood, his muscles ached through inactivity.

The protector shuffled jangling his chains behind him. He pulled at his chains, they were securely imbedded into the wall, bound around his ankles by a tiny lock. He spread his wings and arched his back in a long stretch. How can the images he has shown me actually prove the Enlightened have not lost their focus on the plight of man? Malach shook his head, Lucifer would answer his questions the next time he visited.

Cameron woke with a start, the noise and hubbub of his dormitory stirred him from his sleep as the boys steadily rose, voices rising as more and more boys joined in with the chorus of bird song filtering through the open windows. Cameron rubbed his eyes, a fresh collection of sleep had collected in the corners of his eyelids. He licked his lips and gave a dry swallow. Stiffly he scrambled out of bed and grabbed his soap bag, digging out his toothbrush and toothpaste.

'Morning Cam.'

'Hello Josh' replied Cameron with a smile, pleased to hear Josh greet him once again in the morning.

'Did you sleep ok?' Josh's words muffled by his toothbrush sticking out of the side of his mouth.

'Yeah not bad. I had another dream and I saw....' Cameron stopped himself. Now was not the time to regale Josh with his vision of the night. It would wait. Cameron was now absolutely sure what he had seen was real. Well as real as not being real could be.

'What did you see?' asked Josh.

'Oh nothing, I'll tell you about it later, let's get dressed. I am starving.'

Josh nodded emphatically, leading the sound of his

rumbling stomach towards the washrooms.

Cameron walked down the long aisles in the library. Row upon row of books covered every topic. Fiction, history, geography, applied mathematics, and sports. As he wandered up and down the aisles looking for the language section, he crunched on a hard slice of toast which had been cooked long before the boys had woken. Cameron placed the slice of toast in his blazer pocket, he could smell the full English breakfast accompanying Josh's incredulous words of refusal when Cameron had asked him if he wanted to go to the library with him. The language section was vast, mainly covering European languages such as French, Spanish and German. Cameron found the Latin section at the far end of the aisle, the small light on the wall barely bright enough to make the titles on the spines readable. He looked along the selection of leather bound books, some held well worn spines, the gold embossed lettering looking tired. A brief time learning Latin in his first years at Byford, had now been forgotten. Cameron took the opportunity to drop Latin for extra sports curricula, a decision he momentarily regretted. He tried to remember the words that appeared on the paper within his dream but struggled, so he chose two books which seemed appropriate. Latin for beginners, a small pocket sized book which he decided would be useful if he kept it with him at all times; in case he remembered any of the words during the day. The second book was a large leather bound, Latin to English Encyclopaedia, musty smelling with pages delicate and foxed with age.

    Well that will do for a start he thought, as he returned to the dormitory to put the books safely in his locker he thought of the appearance of the man he saw when he woke from his dream. Was it just my imagination? Not this time, Cameron knew what he saw was real. He wondered why he was not frightened by him, normally he would have been; but there was something about it which made him feel slightly stronger, no not stronger he thought, familiar, yes it felt familiar. Cameron decided he would not acknowledge him should he return, maybe talking to him scared him off. Cameron chuckled to himself at the thought of himself not being scared but the figure standing at the end of his bed being so, he chuckled louder drawing attention of some of the boys as he walked through the corridors to his class.

Chapter Nine

Zahabriel knew the Chief of the Heavenly Armies was right, they had to know what force The Fallen had assembled within The Forest of Wandering Spirits and beyond. Michael deep in thought knew it would be an extremely dangerous mission, but he needed the information; he had to send a scout out to see what lay hidden within the trees. The Fallen had now placed themselves between the angel city and the conduit into man's world, they would have to be pushed back and soon.

'We must know what is going on Zahabriel, whatever the cost!' Michael could see the words strike deep within the cavalry commander.

'Yes sire. The only problem is how to get to the forest without being seen.'

'The only route which may give you the opportunity to approach unseen would be to follow the River Nephesh from the city wall across the kingdom and into the forest, it is going to be difficult. You cannot take a unicorn, this must be done on foot. Even on the wing you would be seen far in advance. Zahabriel I cannot ask for anyone to volunteer for this mission, I could not accept someone volunteering themselves for this assignment knowing the risks. I must take full responsibility. You are ordered to bring back the information we need to assess what we are up against.'

Michael knew Zahabriel's experience would be invaluable

in ultimately carrying the mission through. He was a trooper during the 1st and 2nd Battle of Zo-Har, he had been on the walls of the kingdom when the Enlightened had been on the brink of defeat. Man's world had defeated the evil enveloping the nations, this surge of rejoicing powered the Enlightened into one last thrust to throw The Fallen back to their dark city. Zahabriel had seen at first hand the ferocity and cruelty which The Fallen could unleash.

'One final thing before you go Zahabriel. I would take someone along with you. There will be a better chance of one of you getting back if anything was to go wrong.' Michael went to walk away 'I will leave you to choose who, I will await your return.'

Michael strode away past the Falls of the Divine.

'Now listen carefully, we stay close to the river bank. As we draw nearer to the forest it is vital we don't make any noise at all. Understood?'

Harial acknowledged with a nervous nod, he was the smallest angel within the cavalry cohort, his divining quality Zahabriel had thought. All the troopers were highly trained and experienced. Zahabriel walked up and down the lines of unicorn troopers, all were highly skilled soldiers. Harial had drawn the short straw purely because he was the runt of the troop.

'We do not return until we are certain we have seen all of their forces. We are going to do this once and once only, and then get back in one piece.' Zahabriel gripped the hilt of his sword, he had ordered the trooper to leave all his uniform behind, they both felt very exposed in their white tunics and skirts. Anything that would make a noise or possibly glint in the rays of the Aleph, betraying their presence, was to be left behind.

The two troopers left the security of the city behind them and began to crawl steadily through the edge of the river hugging the bank closely. Zahabriel periodically brought the two of them to a halt. They sat down in the river, it's cool waters going unnoticed as every ripple sounded like a torrent which would surely alert The Fallen, bringing them surging over the top of the bank at them. Zahabriel stretched his neck as hard as he could to try and peer over the crest, the forest still seemed so far away. A wave of his hand and they continued on their tentative journey.

'Surely they would have someone looking over the river?' Harial whispered nervously.

'Well trooper we will find out shortly, now be quiet!' Zahabriel replied, all his senses craning to hear the first signs of warning that they had been discovered.

'You would though sir!'

Zahabriel crouched down and turned to face the trooper making sure that his words did not have to be any louder than they needed.

'I know I would! But these guys are not me are they? We will find out soon enough if they have been as thorough as the Enlightened. But with all the noise you are making they probably realised posting sentries was a waste of time!' Zahabriel turned his head towards the forest, he could not make out any signs of movement and turned back to the trooper. 'Now be quiet!'

'Yes sir' Harial replied frowning at his own nervousness.

Zahabriel felt a slight pang of sympathy for Harial's concern. The trooper was right to expect a strong sentry presence, an impenetrable cordon which would soon spot the two troopers and bring about a swift death.

'Ok, lets get on with it. Sitting here wasting time is only going to get us caught. Now keep your senses tight!' Zahabriel waved his hand and began crawling forward.

The tree line appeared quiet, too quiet. The river as far as Zahabriel could see was not guarded. They have either been very negligent or they are very confident he thought as he stared through the gloom of the tree line. His senses sought out any movement or noise which gaveaway The Fallen's presence. Zahabriel waved, Harial swallowed hard and followed; looking to his left and right, frantically seeking out danger. As they broke through into the forest, the shadowy murk closed in around them. Harial could not have believed as he drove his unicorn back towards the safety of the city when they were ambushed, that he would have been returning so soon. Without his unicorn, or his armour and creeping through the water like a fish.

The forest was eerily silent, no bird song, no rustling of leaves. Zahabriel noted the complete lack of absence of any breeze at all, a strange sensation. Now the breeze was gone, the bird song, even the gentle movement of the trees he realised it was something he had taken for granted. They moved cautiously deeper into the forest following the river bank, in the distance they could make out the roar of the giant falls, the conduit. Harial tapped Zahabriel's shoulder and pointed towards a group of dancing lights, souls waiting for their call back to man's world. A comforting feeling ebbed through the two troopers as some normality was evident within the oppressive gloom.

Zahabriel knew the clearing where he had made a stand against the ambush was just through the cluster of trees immediately in front of him but the trees were too dense for him to see through. He tentatively raised his head above the bank's edge, his fingers biting into the earth as his body was gripped with tension.

'Damn! I can't see a thing!' he muttered under his breath.

Harial joined him peering through the shadows and tree trunks. A sudden noise made them freeze. The tree line was approximately ten feet away from the river bank, in the darkness a scraping noise followed by the sounds of chewing and snapping of twigs. Harial glanced over to his captain, he mouthed for the trooper to stay quiet, Harial did not need telling nodding in acknowledgement. The chewing noises became more frantic, Zahabriel dug his fingers deeper into the ground as he urged his body to rise just a little higher; he needed to see what was just beyond the grassy bank.

He froze as a movement just in front of him caught his eye, the tail of a black wolf jittered from side to side. It walked backwards jerking it's powerful body with each step. As the wolf entered the dim light in front of the tree line, Zahabriel could now make out its defined muscular haunch. It edged backwards. Harial took a deep intake of breath, a gasp that seemed to travel throughout the forest and the kingdom itself. Zahabriel instinctively pushed Harial down into the water, he gulped as the heavy set frame of his captain pressed down on him. Harial struggled. Zahabriel placed his hand tight over the troopers mouth, pressing hard, gesturing with his face for the trooper to calm down. Harial under the powerful grip, regained some control. He took some deep breaths.

'Th...That was an angel wing!' he stammered.

'Shhhh calm down!' Zahabriel pleaded.

Zahabriel pressed down on Harial, urging them both to blend into the bank. He could hear the wolf sniffing the air, his padded footsteps came closer; then they would stop and the wolf once again sniffed. Zahabriel closed his eyes tight. The wolf's heavy panting was now just above him. Harial wide eyed could just make out the outline of the wolf's massive jaws against the dark canopy high above.

Michael sat in his small private chamber, he kept the door slightly ajar, the reassuring throb of the Falls of the Divine swirled in the distant regions of his mind. He sat on a small chair, similar in style to his throne on the dais. The voices of the boys angelic choir entered through the small window, he listened as he stared out at the brilliant blue sky, candles on the small window flickered. Michael looked up as Gabriel knocked softly on the door and entered.

'Penny for them' Gabriel smiled and laughed, 'always thought it a strange saying, heard many men say it to one another. Always wondered how they could give away their inner most secrets so cheaply.'

'Quite, but then they have the ability to give away so much very cheaply' Michael replied.

Gabriel could hear the whisper of despair in Michael's voice. It concerned him, Michael was the strength beating within the kingdom, he was the leader of the archangel throne and a member of each of the other five thrones, or councils, the Principalities, the Powers, Virtues, Dominions, and the Thrones council. Michael had a role within the very fabric of angelic duty. The archangels held responsibility over all common angels and protectors. As the Chief of the Heavenly Armies, Michael sat on the top throne within the Powers who provided responsibility and guidance for the heavenly armies. He also sat as a council member of The Principality council which controlled over nations and cities, and The Virtues who were responsible for overseeing the protection of man's faith. He also sat within the council of Dominions who regulated and monitored angelic duties and were ultimately responsible for the maintenance of all the scrolls. Michael sat at the table of the Thrones, the highest council within the angel kingdom, responsible for overseeing everything that occurred within the angel kingdom and upon man's world. Michael was also one of The Collective, the leaders of the six palaces who could stand before the Aleph.

'The yelediym are in fine voice' remarked Gabriel.

'Yes they are' Michael replied.

Gabriel could feel Michael at this point in time would have preferred to be on his own. He lingered, knowing Michael would come round if given a small amount of space. The choir continued to sing, their voices floating throughout the palaces and across the Sea of Souls towards the city.

Michael lifted his head, closed his eyes.

'A reassuring requiem Gabriel.'

As he turned Gabriel saw a deep well of concern within his emerald green eyes. 'We may need to call upon their strength through voice during the coming times. I feel fear!'

Gabriel softly nodded. 'The city is prepared Michael.'

'The question is Gabriel, prepared for what? It is too early to expect Zahabriel to return with news beyond the forest. But without this information, unless The Fallen show their hand, we do not know what we are dealing with. If Zahabriel or his trooper fail to return we will be forced into seeking confrontation before we are ready....'

Gabriel interrupted. 'Unless they are attempting a massive onslaught Michael, what purpose would it serve invading the kingdom and then sitting within the forest?'

'That is my fear, it is a double edged sword. If The Fallen have massed and are readying themselves to attack the city with strength, we will repel them but as we have learnt in the past through bitter cost, it is not going to be easy. But as you rightly question Gabriel, what if they have not entered the kingdom to crush the city walls, what would their purpose be? That purpose is what causes me the most disquiet.' Michael clenched his fist 'We have to know what lies beyond the distant tree line!'

Zahabriel could smell the putrid stank of evil in the wolf's breath. The black beast scratched at the bank's edge, sending clumps of earth onto the back of the cavalry captain and the face of his trooper. Harial shook his head, straining with all his nerve not to cough and splutter. Zahabriel could feel fear surge into the trooper's body, he was a coiled spring ready to flee as soon as the captain released his grip.

The wolf growled, swiftly turned as he heard his quarry being dragged off back into the forest; the unicorn troopers heard in the near distance the bay of madness as two dark shades fought over the ragged feathered prize.

Zahabriel realised the opportunity to move was now or never. He whispered calmly to Harial, he knew for the sake of both of their lives he had to get his trooper composed. The Sable Wolves were obviously the vanguard of the Sable Core, allowed to roam free, seeking out any would be intruders or any other foolish visitors. They would not be easily swayed to take us as prisoners either Zahabriel pondered, knowing if they were discovered the punishment would be merciless. To try and hide any hint of a scent which could be picked up, the troopers crawled as much as possible within the river's edge.

Zahabriel gestured for Harial to stop, he rested against the bank and peered up towards the tight mass of criss-crossed branches. He could hear his comrades deep breaths as the noise of the wolves fighting over their quarry died way in the distance. The troopers had penetrated deep into the forest, in their eagerness to get away from the dark beasts they had not been scouting the immediate area. They now registered the sounds of activity which permeated throughout the surrounding environment. Zahabriel did not need to look over the river bank, he knew they were now right on the outskirts of The Fallen forces. He nudged Harial with his elbow, looking around craning his neck as far as it would go trying to see what dangers lay behind him.

'If we panic now trooper we are history! It would appear we are in the midst of darkness. We need to get a good look at what is going on and get out of here as quickly, and silently as possible.' His head was facing away from Harial who could just make out the whispered words, the next few he heard perfectly. 'If we get this wrong, do not be taken alive!'

Chapter Ten

Cameron had been impatient all day for the stars to cross a blackened sky. The moonlight gently brightened the dormitory. Before he drifted off to sleep, he had noticed the shadowed figure which seemed to have made a habit of visiting him at night, sitting on top of the great grandfathers clock standing in the corner. Cameron had not drawn any attention to the fact he could see him. Cameron was sure he had seen a cloak, and the white emblem of a knife with what appeared to be wings either side of it on the figures chest, but could not be completely sure. His eyes had become heavy, refusing to be forced open he fell into sleep and rushed towards the vision.

The old man dipped his feathered quill into the inkpot, the pot was almost dry and his ink stained fingers lifted it to drain the remnants of ink to one side, he scraped the quill through the miniscule pool that remained... The vision within his dream continued as it always did... *The old man scratched a few words, placed the feather into its holder in the wooden table, and took the ink pot over to the window where a small metalled jug stood on the window sill. He opened the window a little wider and looked down onto a large square... The old man returned with the small ink pot brimming with fresh black ink. He placed it back into its holder in the desk, and collected the heap of parchment knocking them together bringing all the page edges into a neat alignment.* Cameron could see a paragraph of writing which appeared to be the first page on a pile of papers. The Latin text flowed down the parchment. The elegant lettering was difficult for Cameron to read initially. He trained his eye upon each single word attempting to fix it firmly in his mind. Before he had a chance to get halfway down the first page the vision moved on.

The old man placed the collection of writings on the desk and started to turn each page, browsing quickly through the dancing swirl of letters; he finally came to the last page, placed it up side down on the others, then reached for a blank piece of parchment and began to scratch away dipping the parched quill into the ink pot...

Cameron stirred, blinking his eyes without actually seeing anything. He turned pulling his quilt snugly around his shoulders and slept once more.

Jetrel rubbed his chin, the old man certainly needed to get out more he thought all writing and no play makes him, how do the entities say, boring! The dark angel struggled to see many of the words within the vision. Cameron had stirred too quickly, dimming the images before he could imprint them into his mind. He jumped down onto the floor, and wandered around the dormitory, he started to mischievously walk through the beds, disturbing the souls of the boys; they twisted and turned but their dreams held them asleep. He kept part of his mind attentively within Cameron's in case he returned to the vision. To the side of the boy's dormitory a long bench was fixed on the wall. Jetrel sat down and looked to his left and right along the length of the room. The dormitory held twenty boys, each had a cupboard and a sideboard placed either side of their bed. He probed the tip of his wing into the dust speckled moon rays, cutting shadowed patterns on the dark varnished wooden floor. With a blink of his eyes the moon had crossed the sky and was sinking beyond the horizon. Cameron had not revisited the vision during the night, Jetrel knew he would be waking shortly, time for some air he thought, cutting through the window he soared towards Crawford Lake.

Cameron sat in the library, he had fidgeted throughout his lessons eager to begin work on the passage he had seen in his vision. The library was the quietest room in the school at this time of the day, the majority of the pupils finding any excuse to avoid doing their homework at the expense of other more interesting activities that kept them occupied. Cameron wrote down a few of the words he could remember from his dreams, unsure of whether they were actually correct.

'Lacuna per Enoch', he flicked through the Latin dictionaries. Underneath the Latin words he wrote the translated English, 'words by ?'. Cameron struggled to find an English word for 'Enoch' so he placed a question mark in its place for now. He moved onto the next set of words he could remember, 'per monastica theologus quod gubernatio of quem fides' once again he wrote the English words underneath 'by religious theologians and leaders of man's faith.'

Cameron continued to work with the words he could remember, closing his eyes to bring the words to the forefront of his mind. He concentrated trying to block out any disturbances in the background, he heard the large wooden door of the library open and close with a loud squeal as several pupils entered.

'Hello Cam.'

Cameron opened one eye. Josh stood beside the table smiling exposing a row of chocolate covered teeth, the offending chocolate bar with half it's chocolate sucked away held high.

'Thought you would be here. I brought you a Twix.'

'Thanks' Cameron replied.

'Can I help?' Josh twisted his neck in a vain attempt to see what his friend had been working on.

'Erm….no it's ok Josh, I have nearly finished now.'

'Oh, what is it anyway?'

Cameron looked down at the scribbling on his note pad. He explained to Josh he had started to see some of the words which the old man had written in his dreams. Josh pulled over a chair, chewing away on the last bite of his chocolate bar he grabbed the note pad and read what Cameron had written.

'words by ?… by religious theologians and leaders of man's faith…..soldiers of The Fallen…hidden message within his words…? and ? will cast away their fiery chains…flames of destruction…reverence towards the great…'

'What does it mean exactly?' Josh asked puzzled.

'Exactly!' replied Cameron bluntly, 'I don't know Josh. I couldn't remember all of the words. This is only the start, the small bit I could see was one paragraph, the old man is working from a large book and there is a big pile of paper he has written. Doesn't make a lot of sense though does it?'

Cameron read through the small segment of words, none of it had any meaning to him.

'Cam what is this bit about the soldiers of The Fallen? Who are they?' Josh asked.

'Haven't got a clue.'

Josh held up the pad. 'Well we will have to keep working on it every time you have your dream. Blimey I wonder what it will say?'

Josh wide eyed scanned through the words again, as if by reading it over and over the words would blend together and make sense.

'Oh no, look at the time!' Cameron jumped up from his chair, grabbing the pad out of Josh's hand, then gathered the other books under his arm.

'What is it Cam?'

'I am late for my fencing class. I'll catch you later.'

Cameron run off out of the library. Josh stared after him, then noticed Cameron had forgotten to take the Twix bar, he followed him, one half of the chocolate bar already disappearing into his mouth.

Sebastian sat in his study, he had spent the day at the Home Office, the British government were eagerly investigating every avenue in their hunt for the perpetrators of the Canterbury bombings. Picking at a selection of pastries Emily had cooked, he contemplated the ramifications of the released paper which sat in front of him, seeking clues within it to it's origin. The document had been published by an extreme Christian organisation who now threatened retribution for the murder of the Archbishop of Canterbury, a development whilst unsurprising was very unwelcome.

'We, the Christian Guardians are a ministry for all those whose aims are to uphold Christianity as the Faith of the United Kingdom, and to be a voice for Biblical values for all in every aspect of our lives. With God's grace, we seek to analyse current events in the light of scripture, proclaim God's word to all and provide the information which Christians need in order to pray for the love of God and the precious name of our Lord Jesus Christ. We love our fellow man and grieve for those who have not yet found the direction of the Lord and his commandments, for they will be judged. There is no salvation in messianic leaders of faith or nation. The only hope for our dysfunctional nation lies in the spirit of the Lord Jesus Christ. We are mandated to preach the Gospel and no law will stop those who take our faith seriously. The faithful will rise up in recognition of slain and future martyrs. As the custodians of a heritage that dates back through the generations and which shall be preserved, we will protect the tranquillity of the realm which is now under threat, we will seek out the perpetrators of religious intolerance, and bring upon them just retribution!'

Sebastian continued to finger through the several pages which ultimately threatened to preserve the Christian ideals of a nation no matter what the cost. The forthcoming struggle would be taken up by the so called soldier's of Jesus Christ.

He mulled over the ever building tensions festering beneath the individual communities cohabitating within the cities, and isolated rural communities who were now closing their doors to visitors of differing faiths. These were the beginning threads of a tapestry of tit for tat attacks. The question Sebastian could not answer was against who? No one as yet claimed responsibility for the assassination of Pope Steven or the bombing of Canterbury Cathedral. What purpose lay behind the killings? No leads had been discovered from the two bodies which had been found at the scene of either crime. The official report into the autopsies had given rise to more questions than answers. No obvious cause of death could be ascertained, the notes accompanying the bodies had been analysed by the security forces of Italy and the United Kingdom. They had failed to trace any link or clues through the writing style, ink used or the paper written on.

Sebastian continued to nibble on the small parcels of pastry, washed down with a swig of Scotch, he had also been unable to find a link or a probable reason within the reams of paperwork and speeches made by the Pontiff and the Archbishop. Now this. A religious conflict would tear through the very fabric holding society together. Small sparks would ignite an inferno of hatred, spreading throughout the world. In an age where news travelled around the globe instantaneously it would be nigh on impossible to contain any discontent.

Chapter Eleven

Across the huge swathe of felled trees, at the far end of the newly created clearing Zahabriel could see The Fallen's command building. It was a dark blue orb, supported above the ground within the grip of two immense black wings which emerged from the ground, flanked either side by two great banners, black with their white emblem of the dagger and wings. Similar coloured orbs, smaller and not supported away from the ground spread out evenly from the command orb. A vast blanket, so many the cavalry commander could not accurately assess the numbers. Smaller banners evenly spaced, spanned the complete perimeter of their newly built encampment, this was the encampment of The Sable Core.

Luckily for the two troopers, The Fallen were confident they were far from the gaze of any Enlightened angel, no sentries had been posted within the Forest of Wandering Spirits, leaving their beasts to prowl and sniff out any danger. Zahabriel squinted towards the back edge of the clearing, he could just make out the frames of siege weapons, hundreds of them, row upon row. Soldiers milled about between the orbs; reassuringly the troopers could not see any wolves of the Sable Cavalry. Zahabriel wanted to know who was commanding The Sable Core, but he also needed to find out what siege weapons they had brought. He decided this could only be achieved if himself and Harial split up.

'We will fare better if we separate, less chance of us

being discovered.' Zahabriel pointed down along the bank of the river. 'Follow the river a little further down, you will then have to break into the newly created tree line over there and work your way over to the siege weapons. If you need to, fly up into the canopy. But only if you have to, The Fallen seem to be very confident no one would attempt to break into the forest at this moment in time and have not placed any sentries, which is helpful. But, the wolves are roaming free. When you are sure you have seen everything they have, return back here.'

Zahabriel took another glance across the encampment, then turned and sat back down next to Harial.

'I'm going to find out who is leading this rabble. I will return here when I have seen what I need to. Any commotion that signals one of us has been discovered the other must, MUST!' Zahabriel stressed 'get back to the city and report what we have seen. No heroics trying to save the other, if caught there will be nothing that can be done.'

Zahabriel looked at Harial, his head was bowed and he looked into the flowing waters of the River Nephesh.

'Do you understand Harial?'

'Yes sir' Harial replied, Zahabriel looked into the trooper's deep green eyes. The trooper had shown great courage so far, Zahabriel expected nothing less, but this trooper had carried the reputation of the Unicorn Cavalry with great honour.

'Right away you go, be careful, take your time. Make sure your eyes see what you actually see. We need to know what we are up against.'

Zahabriel watched the trooper as he cautiously moved away along the bank of the river. He then turned towards his task, Zahabriel knew he had the riskier of the two missions, but only he would recognise any of The Fallen commanders.

Zahabriel had managed to skirt around the edge of The Fallen camp, he had heard the wolves in the distance prowling within the forest but had thus far avoided getting to close. The command orb now stood directly in front of him, he lay in a hollow between a triangle of trees. The cavalry commander felt very exposed, but all his experience told him he would be impossible to see from the encampment, the gloom of the forest covered him in shadow. The immediate danger would come from behind. The orb was a swirling dark blue mass, steps led up to a doorway that seemed to be a layer of smoke. Either side of the door stood two impressive soldiers of The Sable Guard. Zahabriel saw many dark angels, sitting around their smaller orbs, some were walking around the camp in a relaxed manner. They did not carry their shields or spears but were armed with their swords. Relaxed they even forwent wearing their helmets. Zahabriel could hear them talking amongst themselves but not clearly enough to make out what about, he knew this was as close as he could possibly get to the command orb or the outskirts of The Fallen encampment. To attempt to get any closer would be extremely foolish. He would have to wait, and was reassured to hear no signs of any trouble had emanated from the far side of the camp where Harial was making his way round to scout the siege weapons.

Harial had made good time in scouting around the opposite side of the camp; his commander had been right in his assessment of The Fallen's confidence in not placing any sentries. Harial had seen individual soldiers of The Sable Core within the confines of the encampment, but not one guarding the perimeter. Harial moved in short bursts, then crouched, seeking cover and listening out for any danger, especially from the dark beasts. The siege weapons were now ahead of him, but he needed to get closer to accurately see the particular types of weapons gathered. As Harial crept ever closer he could see dark angels working around the massive armaments. Weapons which would take a heavy toll upon the walls of the angel city, weapons which would fire their projectiles of destruction over the walls into the very city itself.

Harial swallowed hard, he could not individually count them but estimated there were many hundreds.

He could see Arogen catapults, this siege engine was part of The Fallen's heavy artillery. Up to fifty soldiers would use the large handles to the left and rear of the catapult, which would wind the throwing arm back. A cushion of light at the front of the catapult, was there to soften the blow of the throwing arm, preventing the machine from tearing itself apart as it threw the missile skyward. Further along the line Harial could make out the large Stabilla, it was a siege engine used to fire bolts of dark light. It had a shorter range than the Arogen and would be operated by ten dark angels, weapons in the experienced hands of The Sable Core extremely effective against massed ranks of troops.

Harial did not have to move any further down the tree line to make out the Chetuber, immense siege weapons, requiring one hundred soldiers of The Sable Core's artillery divisions to work each piece. Chetubers were not effective against troops or horses, Harial could see these were excellent for smashing walls and gates. The Chetuber had a pivoting lever supported high above the ground by a frame of light. The short end of the lever had a huge black ball which acted as a heavy counterweight, and the long end of the lever had a cradle of dark light, this held an enormous boulder of fire. The Chetuber projectiles would strike the walls of the Enlightened city until they cracked and crumbled, making a hole big enough for large divisions of The Sable Core to pour through. The Chetuber was also capable of firing high over the wall causing immense damage within the city itself.

Harial, now at the very edge of the tree line could see The Fallen could literally envelope the whole of the city wall and bombard it from every angle. He had all information he needed, time to get out of here he thought. The trooper had a brief look round to make sure his route back was clear. When he was confident no sentries had strayed into his section of the perimeter he set off back to the river.

The perimeter remained quiet, he had no trouble in making good progress. As he broke through the tree line, a small group of dancing lights to his right caught his eye, Harial wandered down towards the river bank, watching them as they twirled around each other then shoot into the thick shadows of the forest. In those brief seconds of distraction he had not noticed two dark soldiers kneeling down by the water's edge to his left. They reacted quickly to the noise Harial made as he came into view, the trooper had no time to react. He made a vain attempt to pull his sword from his scabbard, but one of the dark angels swooped from his left, the other came around in front of him and attacked on his right. Harial was knocked from his feet, as he fell he twisted and fell face down. One of the dark angel's brought the shaft of his spear down sharply across the back of Harial's head with a sickening thud.

Zahabriel waited patiently, knowing the longer he stayed, the greater the danger of being discovered. He decided to wait a little longer. If he could see who was in command of The Sable Core, it may give Michael a better idea of their intended strategy and reason for invading through the angel conduit. The camp had remained in a state of calm, not giving the impression of an invading army at all. The banners beside the command orb fluttered gently, there was no breeze but the sheer size and weight of them initiated some movement as they hung from their poles.

Zahabriel was startled by a cry from the far side of the encampment which ran alongside the river. The feathers on his wings tingled. The cry could mean only one thing. He notice a soldier come running across the camp towards the command orb, he ran up the stairs and was abruptly halted by the two guards. Speaking briefly with them, he was allowed to enter, the smoke swirled as he disappeared through the door.

The commotion on the far side grew more frantic, confirming to Zahabriel, if any doubt remained that Harial had been discovered. All his senses urged him to turn and run, The Fallen would now be alerted and would surely send out scouts to hunt down any other spies. He waited a moment longer, his patience and courage were rewarded. The smoky door swirled once more, at the top of the stairs stood the commander of the Sable Core, Dagon.

The captain of the unicorn cavalry stood before Michael in his private chamber, he had received the news from

Zahabriel with a non committal expression. Zahabriel informed him of the size of the force within the forest, the information Dagon was commanding was extremely valuable. Michael knew from bitter experience his adversary was a wily, ruthless commander. A commander who never took any unnecessary risks, his every move always well thought out.

'The information you have returned with captain is most useful' Michael could see the loss of his trooper was biting deep into Zahabriel's angelic soul. 'It will allow us to respond to The Fallen, and plan appropriately. Your mission and the loss of the trooper have not been in vain.'

'No sire, Harial had news of the siege weapons that we observed. Unfortunately I could not see them well enough from my position to accurately assess what type and how many.'

Michael thought for a moment, whilst it would have been advantageous to know exactly what type of siege engine The Fallen had brought and the numbers, it was at least valuable to know they had them. Both Michael and Zahabriel had seen first hand the carnage these weapons caused. Michael raised his hand.

'The knowledge of their presence will suffice.....' Michael was interrupted by a frenzied knock on his chamber door.

'Enter' Michael said sternly.

A frantic herald stepped into the room, he bowed and then stammered out his message. 'S...Sire, the d...duty officer requests you come immediately to the Gates of Arabah!'

Michael could see the summons had not been requested lightly. The messenger was sent on his way. Michael and Zahabriel followed.

When the archangel arrived at the wall above the Gates of Arabah, he saw the soldiers on sentry duty had filtered down towards the gates, and were looking out across the plains towards the Forest of Wandering Spirits. He looked around and up at the two inner walls, they too were now crowded with interested spectators. Michael and Zahabriel glared across the pastures. In front of the forest they could see a large legion of Sable Core standing in a large arc, their tall black oval shields in front of them, the emblem of The Fallen reflecting bright white in the rays of the Aleph. Their white crests on top of their black helmets fluttered gently in the wind. Behind the arc, a group of dark angels could be seen working purposefully.

Very slowly a large five pointed cross was hauled up vertically. On the cross could be seen the crucified figure of Harial. His wings spread wide horizontally, nailed to the horizontal arms of the cross by short swords, his hands nailed above his head. His feet were overlapped, staked through with a large fallen blade. The horns of The Fallen echoed throughout the forest and died away. Michael clenched his fists. Zahabriel dropped his head, unable to look. The voices of the choir of yelediym drifted from the palaces across the Sea of Souls through the streets and lanes of the city, they carried across the green plains as a silence filtered throughout the whole of the kingdom. Michael slowly raised his hand, as one with the drop of the archangel's arm, hundreds of arrows flew in an arc toward the same point above their slain comrade. They all converged to create an illuminescent ball of light which floated down towards the crucified angel, slowly fading away. They had honoured Harial.

Chapter Twelve

A sense of desperation welled within Malach. The orbs on the far side of his cell crackled as the shadows teasingly danced around him, laughing spirits of free will, free to move as they wished. He crouched on the floor, squeezing into a slither of shadow. He had begun to feel tired and worn out, not physically, his body had a weary edge to it from a lack of exercise but it was his mind which took the greatest burden of his imprisonment; he had been visited by Lucifer on many occasions. The discussions tended to be one sided. Malach had seen first hand Lucifer was an extremely charismatic angel, the leader of The Fallen had a very persuasive manner. Malach knew he was out of his depth. Lucifer's words were very difficult to dismiss, it took all of his strength to remain strong and focused upon the path of enlightenment. With every visit either from the dark prince or Samsaweel, who was also a very keen attendant, he was reminded, if any reminder had been necessary, of his predicament with the constant promise of release if he took on the ways and beliefs of The Fallen.

In between the unwelcomed guests, he tried to focus his mind on the world he had left behind, some of the images had started to gradually become foggy. He'd close his eyes, and flew from the world of entities through the conduit into the angel kingdom. The conduit was a fluid gateway, the falls falling between the two peaks were only accessible by the angels; as they travelled through it they could access anywhere they wished within the world of entities. Guarded to keep out the angels and beasts of the dark, but a weak point of the kingdom to a heavy, sustained attack.

He felt the coolness of The Forest of Wandering Spirits, as he strolled along the path he could see the dancing lights, hear the bird song and feel the gentle breeze on his skin. The breeze carried the sweet smell of the green pastures, and in the far distance he was sure he could make out the voices of the palace choir. The winding path cut through the forest, the song of the river audible. As he came to the edge of the tree line, the light became brighter, the green grasses took on a paler edge as he blinked adjusting his eye sight from the gloom. He broke out into the open countryside, in the distance stood the white city. It sat in the caress of a snow tipped mountain. The rays of the Aleph probed outward to all corners of the kingdom.

Malach opened his eyes and shifted his position, he ran his hands roughly through his hair, arching his shoulders back in a taut stretch. He closed his eyes once again.

The tall arch of the Gate of Arabah soared above him as he strolled through into the kingdom, he could hear the snap of the banners high on top of the towers. He wandered through the hurley burley of the city towards the square, the four fountains majestically sprouted flames of dancing water. Amongst the throng, he spotted Seir. She waved softly, mouthing words of greeting, Malach could not hear the spoken words lost in the air. He waved back, and tried to walk towards her, the harder he tried to reach her, the greater the mass of angels that thwarted his efforts. He could see Seir smiling at him, a warming, radiant smile.

Malach opened his eyes, a pressure built within his chest.

He took gulps of breath as a crushing grip of need enclosed around him, realising the feelings of want were increasing both in strength and duration.

He stood and leant against the wall, he closed his eyes again; returning to the city would hopefully help him quell the pain. Seir had gone, with a sigh he turned towards the small lane leading from the square towards the Sea of Souls. The narrow lane ended and opened onto a large garden, deep rustic red Maple trees lined a vast round ornamental pond, containing the kaleidoscope of white, red and black of powerful Koi. Walking around the perimeter of the pond, weaving in and out of the Maple trees, he came to the bank of the Sea of Souls. He sat himself down on the velvet carpet of grass, and stared across the gentle ripples of the sea at the seven palaces, far off into the distance. With a large sigh, he opened his eyes, stared hard into the flames of the becketed torches.

I cannot stay here any longer he thought. I have to get out. I cannot be weak, recruited by The Fallen to forever exist in perpetual damnation. With no chance of forgiveness from the Aleph would be a fate far worse than the light within me fading. Well, there are two obvious routes to take… refuse the succour of Lucifer and ultimately reap his wrath, or escape! Defying Lucifer is the easiest option. How can I escape these walls? Malach clenched his fist and struck the wall.

Josh owned a puzzled frown that stretched deep lines across his forehead. He glanced at Cameron, then at the television, then back to Cameron. The news bulletins were wall to wall coverage on the deepening crisis within the country and parts of the world; a broadcast from a religious sect, claiming responsibility for the murder of Pope Steven and the bombing that destroyed Canterbury Cathedral had sent shock waves throughout the entire world. They claimed the fight would continue to re-establish the one true original faith as the one faith of all men. The news reader read through the transcript sent through to all major news agencies.

'I don't understand Cam, what is the...'

Josh was stopped mid sentence as Cameron held his hand up, gesturing for him to be quiet. Cameron sat on the edge of his chair, his hands clasped together resting on his knees. He was sure his regular companion was sitting on the sofa next to Josh, he could very faintly see the outline of him, the air hazed where he sat. Cameron realised he was able to see him clearer at night time, or was it just the dark? he wondered. I will have to test that out. Cameron returned his attention to the television as the newsreader read out the statement...

'From a Christian viewpoint, God's purpose in establishing the Jewish people was to have them receive the Messiah. Jews throughout time have been perceived as the nation that failed him. Judaism as been regarded as having a defective doctrine of God. We are offended by a Christian misrepresentation of our religion, which can be found throughout the New Testament. They do not see any superiority in Jesus' ethics over that of the best rabbis, who are after all the keeper's of God's teachings and guidance. We question evidence which would bare truth to the fact Jesus was any kind of Messiah. After all, a lack of accomplishment for one who would call himself the Messiah is testament to the deceit which lies within their religious story book. Jesus the 'so called' Messiah has left a world filled with violence and oppression, and for the one true faith it grew much worse. His presence among man was the starting-point for the legacy of Christian anti-Semitism. Eons of Christian violence against Jews: mob violence, pillaging, rape, confinement to ghettos, forcible abduction of children to be baptized as Christians, expulsions from many nations and finally the Holocaust. Christian anti-Semitism is the sword which has speared the life of tens of millions of people who lived and died through that persecution. The leaders of the Christian faith have aligned themselves with Catholicism. We have struck in defence of our faith, the original faith, the faith given to man by God. All other faiths are the hybrids of man's self driven road to power and rule. All other faiths are a play upon the one true faith. Ultimately they are all meaningless, heretic societies that will be wiped from the conscience of man!'

'Blimey what a mouthful!' claimed Josh.

'A mouthful? That is exactly what I have been talking about Josh,' replied Cameron, 'well to a point.' Cameron thought for a moment. 'Answer me this Josh. If you was God...'

'Yes' said Josh, still frowning.

'...and you had created everything, would you allow people to go and pray to someone else?'

Josh deep in thought puckered his lips, he always did this when an intelligent answer was needed.

Cameron continued, '...would you allow all the wars to happen? And all the starving people? The need for charity and all that?'

Josh's pucker became more pronounced.

'No' he replied.

'Exactly! That is what I have been saying over the past few months. If there was a God why would he allow it all to go wrong?'

Jetrel nodded appreciatively, he sat next to Josh, relaxed back in the deep comfortable upholstery. His arm out stretched on the back of the sofa, crossed legged he listened to the boys exchange views upon the existence of God and heaven. He watched as the entities on the television poured over, analysed then re-analysed his piece of handy work.

Cameron lay in his bed, the sounds of sleep surrounded him. A few restless bodies squirmed under their duvets as they urged sleep upon them. He stared up into the ceiling, his hands behind his head. He wiggled his toes to free the tightness around them caused by his heavy quilt. He wondered if the vision would return tonight, where once he dreaded falling asleep in case he entered the dream with the old man, he would now wake and become frustrated if the old man did not appear. He was impatient to finish the passage, to reveal what the old man had been writing.

Cameron became disturbed from his thoughts by Jetrel roaming around the room. Who is he? Cameron wondered. He had decided it was the dark which made him easier to see, during the day when it was light, his image was replaced by the hazy air that accompanied his presence.

He thought about the news bulletin he and Josh had sat through, his parents had encouraged him to question rather than to just except things at face value. It would be at times like these he would sit down with his mother especially, as Cameron's father was normally away, and discuss many things. No topic appeared to be beyond her, which always amazed him. He swallowed the suffocating lump growing in his throat, time had not healed the wound. When he was occupied, he had begun to manage to push her to the back of his mind, but during quiet times, especially just before he fell asleep, he would go over what the day had brought. It was at these moments he wished she was around, just to share his thoughts. Cameron thought about the meaning of his existence. What did it all mean in the end? His mother used to say everyone had a path, dreams to fulfill, if you allowed yourself. But many people chose a path guided by forces which led them astray, they could always resume the right path if they so wished, but never quite in the same way had they continued down the pathway without any deviation.

Cameron shook his head, as Josh mumbled some words replaying his dream for all to hear. So what was her destiny? Cameron thought, where did her path lead to? She was taken, I can't see how she was able to fulfill anything that she would have wanted to do. Cameron became angry, he had so many questions, and no answers. If only he could talk to her, just for the briefest of moments.

Jetrel heard Cameron's thoughts, and decided to sit on the wooden bench at the side of the wall, near the window where the moon's rays would strike through. He listened to Cameron's pain. Cameron's mind was wide open, Jetrel had no problems seeing through.

Emily says mum is with me all the time, all I need to do is talk to her and she will hear me. How do I know if she can hear me? If she can hear me, why is it I cannot hear her? Unless Emily is wrong and mum is not with me at all.

Cameron took a deep breath, letting out a long gentle

sigh. A tear fell down the side of his face, collecting inside his ear which made it itch; he probed his finger inside drying the water away. Cameron struggled to stop the tears welling up in his eyes, blurring the deep gloom within the room. A vice of hurt gripped his whole being, he shuddered as he attempted to stem the cry. He swallowed hard several times, rubbing his eyes and face with the palms of his hands. If mum cannot be with me, who is the figure that is always around? Cameron lifted his head and looked around, Jetrel heard the words. As a ghost they might know where mum is, and why do they stay with me. It isn't a school ghost, seems to be my ghost. When the time seems right I will talk to it again. With another shudder and a deep sigh, he rolled over grabbing the duvet and pulling it tight around his shoulders, he closed his watery eyes and drifted into sleep.

Jetrel pondered over Cameron's words, he knew the entity without any doubt was aware of his presence. This entity was far beyond his years. Jetrel now realised the boy was deliberately shying away from making contact, waiting until he felt Jetrel would be receptive. The dark angel was stirred from his thoughts as he saw the old man emerge into sight, Cameron was dreaming.

....The old man returned with the small ink pot brimming with fresh black ink. He placed it back into its holder in the desk, and collected the heap of parchment knocking them together bringing all the page edges into a neat alignment.

Once again at this point in the dream Cameron could see the writing. The Latin verse became clearer, underneath he could see more passages of writing expand. Numbers amongst the sentences stood out.

The old man placed the collection of writings on the desk and started to turn each page, browsing quickly through the dancing swirl of letters, he finally came to the last page....a sudden intense flash of light interrupted the dream....Cameron was suddenly flying above snow crested mountains, heavy grey snow filled clouds sat low on their peaks. He approached the side of one of the cluster of mountains. Below, he could see six black dots moving tentatively along an icy ledge. As the vision drew Cameron closer to the mountain side he could now see the black dots were actually six horseman. Through the heavy blizzard he could see the fourth horseman was a knight, similar to the one he had seen on the ship. A box wrapped in cloth was strapped to his horse's rump. The wind howled, driving the biting cold and snow into the horsemen's faces. They gripped the reins tightly knowing a slip would send them hurtling hundreds of feet to their death. Beneath their horses they began to feel the mountain shake, the horsemen looked towards the peak. Dumbstruck they saw a wall of snow hurtling towards them, it's roar boomed above the wind. The two lead horsemen were swept from the ledge by the force of air being blown forward before the avalanche. The remaining horsemen squeezed themselves tight into the mountain face, a futile attempt as they were swallowed up, falling into the cavernous gorge below...another intense flash of light brought Cameron back to the old man, he browsed out of the open window then continued to write a few more sentences. The quill scratched neat flamboyant lettering, a sip of wine then a return to his work. The old man turned towards the door, a knock had disturbed him. He gingerly rose from the wooden chair, his muscles and bones tight from sitting for long periods in the same *position. He pulled the heavy wooden door open, a small man stood with a handful of parchments, Cameron was now standing in the corridor, a narrow stone walled corridor lined with torches......he turned back to the door, which slammed shut...*

Cameron stirred slightly but sleep continued to hold him. Jetrel had seen part of the passage. Languages were the creation of man, angels were able to hear and read any language in the tone of their own angelic language. If only the boy could stay focused on the vision for longer periods, he thought, although Samsaweel will be most interested to hear the boy has seen through to the writings.

From experience he knew Cameron would not return back to the vision, he looked around, with a smile he knelt down by the bed of one of Cameron's friends. With his finger he gently flicked the boys earlobe, an angel chuckle crackled throughout the room, he laughed as the boy in his sleep state tried to swat the annoyance away with his hand.

For Josh and Cameron the day could not end quick enough. Cameron had rushed away from his fencing class, he would have normally stayed behind and worked on his technique a little longer, but this evening he wanted to work on the passage. He had written down the words he could remember as soon as he woke, he still struggled to remember the whole thing, but he had added a few more words to the gaps.

'Right let's see what we have got now' Cameron said as he scanned the words he had written.

'Read each word out Cam, and I will look it up' Josh said enthusiastically.

Cameron held the pad up and gave Josh the first set of new words.

Josh read through the Latin books, flicking through the pages searching for each individual word. When he found it he scribbled down what he had discovered frantically. Cameron lay on the bed next to him, patiently waiting for his friend to reveal what he had uncovered.

'Have been ordered hidden' Josh informed Cameron with an air of achievement.

Cameron wrote the English translation under the equivalent Latin words.

'Right ok, the next lot I think is Pro illa lacuna habitum a if that is how you pronounce it.'

Josh again scribbled the words down.

'For these words hold a..' Josh said.

Cameron worked through two more sections he had written, together they sat and looked at the words.

'words by ? have been ordered hidden by religious theologians and leaders of man's faith.....soldiers of The Fallen.....hidden message within his words. For these words hold a...The two originators of...? and ? will cast away their fiery chains...flames of destruction. Then the new creation of...reverence towards the great...'

'How much more is there Cam?'

Cameron looked puzzled at the disjointed words.

'Well as far as I can tell Josh a fair bit. This is just the first paragraph I saw, there is a massive pile of paper that the old man has been writing!'

Cameron went on to tell Josh about the knights upon the mountain who had appeared. His best friend listened intently, excited about their sudden demise. He informed Cameron where they had gone wrong. Their first and most important mistake, leading to an expedition which was doomed to failure right from the outset, was not having him as a member of the bodyguard. Whatever the boxes were, it seemed they were surely important enough to have an escort. Cameron laughed, he could see how both expeditions were seriously lacking Josh's leadership qualities.

The knights were another part of the confusing puzzle but for now Cameron decided it was important to concentrate on deciphering the text. The two boys read through and re-read the mish mash of words. None of it made any sense to them. Cameron knew he would have to work on remembering more of the text in his dream.

The Fallen City was created by the will of the original fallen angels, Azazel, Semhaza and Lucifer. Cast from the angel kingdom along with two hundred angels who decided to follow, the original three had to find a home amongst men. Their existence to be forever in the midst of those who they failed to serve. Upon arriving on earth they focused all of their mind's energies, the Fallen City formed through their assembled power within the very heart of the earth itself. The dark angels always assisted man in his belief the core of their world was a furnace of molten rock. A swirling mass that is the fulcrum of the earth's rotation.

Samsaweel felt it was time to call upon Jetrel and see how he was faring with the entity. But before he would grace the daemon with his presence, it had been a while since he had visited the Fallen's current house guest.

He walked through the stoned corridors, lit by evenly spaced dark blue orbs of pulsating light which emanated a brighter light far greater than their colour would suggest.

The sombre, walled make-up of the city was in direct contrast to the orb of energy surrounding it. Malach's cell was situated deep inside the city. The archangel strolled through the maze of corridors which interconnected the living areas of the kingdom. As he approached the cell, the guard outside snapped to attention, he made to enter the room when the guard coughed under his breath. Samsaweel stopped, gave him a look that burnt into the side of his face.

'Well!' snapped Samsaweel impatiently.

The guard kept his gaze straight ahead.

'I thought you would like to know the Prince is inside with the Enlightened one.'

Samsaweel was not surprised Lucifer was paying Malach another visit, he had spent a lot of time with the protector. He smirked, this may be a fine moment to inform Lucifer he was on his way to visit the boy and Jetrel.

'Samsaweel' said Lucifer without turning round. 'Welcome to our little soirée.'

Malach gave the dark archangel a contemptuous look.

'My Prince' Samsaweel said with a deep bow.

Lucifer kept his gaze on Malach and spoke to Samsaweel.

'What do we owe the pleasure of this visit?'

'Sire I thought you might be interested to know that I am off to visit the daemon who accompanies the boy. Progress has been made.' Samsaweel said focusing on Malach's reaction.

'Excellent news. See protector, the boy has appeared to have suffered no ill effects through the partnership with the so called dark side. It just needs a little guidance and the opportunity to show man that the path to the great light offers them ultimately no inner happiness. Our daemon has achieved more in the months he has accompanied him than you did in fourteen of his years.'

Malach took a deep breath, 'I know not how you have achieved your so called success with Cameron, but I am sure it is through subterfuge. The boy would never follow the dark road, through free will. The play on his mind is the only way you could gain access to him. As is the way of all men, yes there are many who are weak and will follow your trail to chaos. Those who are stronger, those entities who would not succumb through free will, they are coerced…'

Lucifer took a step forward.

Malach stepped back as Lucifer's growl drove deep into him.

'You think oh Enlightened one that the Aleph does not coerce, as you so eloquently put it. The words of the Bridge Makers, you shalt not do this, you shalt do that. Repent your sins or else! Those who will bow down on his knees in the beauty of his presence will forever find peace and light. Those who refuse will be forever cast into the fire of damnation! Don't preach to me young one about the art of coercion.'

'The dark's version of coercion is to spread fear,' Malach replied 'the feeling of abandonment. You showed me the image of urchins and men working in pitiful conditions, you made a big play upon the turned cheek of the light. It is the leaders of these men who are guided by your angels, spreading the wealth of nations, in a way which keeps the people they supposedly serve in abject poverty, subservient to the minority of dark led entities claiming the riches for themselves. It is men who lead other men, guiding the path of nations. They have the greatest impact on hope or despair, wealth or poverty, honour or eternal damnation. Those guided by your hand revel in the shadows of their fellow man's pain and misery.'

Lucifer laughed, bringing a chill over Samsaweel.

'Where are the Enlightened ones protector? Those who would be fighting the corner of the suppressed many against the privileged few. These few which are guided by my hand. Ask yourself that. The tides of power within man's world is changing. It is I and my forces who are winning the hearts of all. All those who oppose the coming change in hierarchy will feel my wrath. Join us Malach and be for ever rewarded with a seat by my side.'

'Join you Lucifer? I have been told of the great battles between The Fallen and the Enlightened. Legions of angels interlocked in death throws in the skies above men. Through the ages when man has fought each other; above them clash the armies of angels. When they cry 'For God!' how little do they realise the forces at play. The last great war of men, a war guided by the hand of your dark forces almost brought the light to their knees. But, through the will and strength of both men and angels, your quest failed. It will always fail Lucifer. It will fail because of entities like the urchins and beggars you showed me. Their strength of heart and inner belief will always prevail. Join you Lucifer? Never!'

Lucifer roared, Malach hit by a force, the like he had never felt before, flung him through the air slamming him into the wall. The air exploded from his lungs. He slumped to the floor, a white haze floated before his eyes. Through the fog, Malach saw the shadow of the dark prince leaving the cell. Samsaweel stepped forward and bent over the protector mockingly.

'I do not think he was too happy with your little speech Malach! You have been very foolish. The coercion you speak of has provided your entity to us. You see it only takes a small gesture to prove the doubt in the back of most entities minds is real.'

Samsaweel was outwardly enjoying the moment.

'When they realise they are alone, that their prayers fall upon deaf ears, then why would they not come over to the side who will guide them to achieve all that is possible. The boy is unique amongst his kind, he holds within him qualities any protector worthy of guiding him would have seen.'

It was a slight which drove deep into Malach.

'He has a strong, inner spirit. A will which needed to be weakened to allow us to probe his belief. So, we took his mother!'

Samsaweel paused, making sure the protector had understood the significance of what he had said.

'Yes we conveniently arranged the car accident. The lorry driver momentarily distracted by a daemon, never saw the red traffic light or the boy's mother's car. He now feels not only the pain and loss all entities inevitably feel at these times, but he rightly questions. Where was the Aleph? What was the purpose of her death? The answer Malach, coercion!'

Chapter Thirteen

Michael sat at the thick marbled table with the other members of The Collective Council, situated in the palace of The Aleph. Michael, representing the council of Archangels and Powers, sat opposite Asiel; the council leader of the Virtues was a chubby angel. His round face swallowing up his small, sparkly eyes. His rotund girth giving the impression he was smaller than he really was. To his left sat Gadriel council leader of Principalities. Large even by The Powers standard, his massive frame was carried with the poise of a leader whose calculating political skills were well respected. Uslael sat on Michael's right, the leader of the Dominion council, carried boyish looks which belied the passage of time which had passed since he served within the ranks of the protectors. Never able to remain still, he constantly scratched his chin or pushed his hand through his mousy, brown hair. Next to Calliel, the council leader of the Thrones; a calm, squat angel, whose reflective analysis of any subject would always bring a voice of reason, sat Zephaniel consort to the Aleph. Zephaniel held the Trident of the Kingdoms, it's three prongs of light represented honour, insight and servitude; the core elements which defined their duty to the kingdom of man. He set it's short staff into the table in front of him leaving only the head of the trident visible. The Collective could now begin.

The table sat on an island of pearl blue light, crystal

waters surrounded the platform. A soft ripple danced across the water, caused by the fountains arching away from the backs of the council member's chairs. Each chair, the sculpted frame of a unicorn, their horns pointed skyward, representing the Atarah of the kingdom. Water gushed from the unicorn's open mouths, the life force of the universe. The two prancing front hooves represented the majestic power of the angel kingdom.

'What force lies within the Forest of Wandering Spirits, Michael?' Zephaniel leant on the table his fingers interlocked. His stern chiselled features were a picture of reflective concern.

'A sizeable force. Estimated at four legions at least. They have brought siege engines with them, I believe they pose a very serious threat to the kingdom.' Michael glanced at each of the council members in turn. 'They are led by Dagon himself!'

'I see....' replied Zephaniel. 'Can we be sure Dagon is present?'

'He was seen by Zahabriel.'

Zephaniel nodded. The cavalry commander was very well respected. Zephaniel knew Zahabriel would not have reported the sighting of the dark commander unless he was certain it was him.

'Any thoughts about what our response should be?'

Michael pondered, 'as I see it we have two obvious choices. The first, we strike immediately, hit them hard, push them back through the conduit. Force them to engage outside of the realm. The second, is do nothing, yet. We wait!'

The council members turned towards each other, each owned a puzzled gaze.

'What would we achieve by waiting?' questioned Uslael. 'Surely by striking fast and hard we give ourselves a greater chance of pushing The Fallen back, before they become entrenched within the forest.'

'Yes that would seem the sensible option,' Michael replied 'and given any other circumstance one I would support...'

'But?' interrupted Zephaniel. He sat back in his chair, his elbows rested on the arms, his hands clasped with his two forefingers caressing his lips thoughtfully.

'But...I do not believe The Fallen are here on an isolated plan of attacking the city walls and invading the realm.' Michael spoke, with a less than convincing tone. 'The dark forces have never forced their hand against us without splitting our resources amongst the world of the entities. I cannot see this being an isolated move.'

'The Bridge Makers! The slaying of the two Bridge Makers is causing considerable religious turmoil around the world...' said Asiel. 'The leaders of the Juda faith have been energised in denouncing the claims that followers of a fanatical wing of Judaism were responsible for the assassination of Pope Steven and the attack on the cathedral of Canterbury. In cities, attacks on religious buildings, districts and individuals are now creating pressures on governments to come down on the church councils. The fabric of societies are strained. The Fallen have mobilised their Virtues.'

'The dark Principalities have also mobilised confirming Asiel's observation regarding the nation's governments.' Confirmed Gadriel. 'Several sable guided leaders have taken this opportunity to drive a wedge between the faith of men they feel are weak and so are able to persecute. Or, to target the stronger factions which if removed would increase their hand of power.'

'It would be prudent to be guarded against fallen guided leaders moving across their borders and making moves onto foreign lands' stated Calliel, 'a spark which would once again benefit the dark roads to chaos.'

Zephaniel continued to scratch his bottom lip with his forefinger. 'So it would appear The Fallen's viper is not a single headed strike upon us.'

'My concern Consort, is how many heads does this viper have?' added Michael.

The Collective Chamber thrummed to the six fountains of water. Six guards, one in each corner of the room and two by the huge doors stood like statues, holding their spears at a slant, their tall shields reflecting the light of the room into long rays that met in the centre of the room. Over the council table.

'You do not speak with a secured conviction Michael when questioning The Fallen's plans' said Zephaniel.

'Consort, as we have heard, it would seem The Fallen are working on many fronts. Their usual strategy of splitting our resources into isolated forces, knowing our strength lies as one, is obviously at work.'

'But?' interceded Zephaniel again.

'But....' Michael paused 'that is the dilemma, my dilemma! I am not certain The Fallen have committed themselves fully yet. Hence why they wait within the forest.'

'True....' replied Gadriel 'you have a point, why would they wait within the tree line? If the cavalry commander has seen the massed forces you state, plus their siege weapons, what is the purpose of delay?'

'If your assumption is correct Michael, how many heads of this.....viper.....are there? asked Uslael.

'More importantly, where or why will it strike?' added Calliel.

Asiel leant forward, shifting his bottom awkwardly. 'If we decide to wait, are we prepared for any move that The Fallen may make? The current situation shows they have carried through their predictable strategies, targeting the entities in conjunction with a move against the realm. They have struck at man's faith, mobilising the Virtues. They have struck at nation's leaders, mobilising the Principalities. Their legions have massed to strike at our walls.'

'So where else could they move against?' asked Gadriel. 'We have mobilised the Virtues and Principalities in direct response, what could they be waiting for...where else could they strike?'

Michael spoke sternly. 'Within the city walls!'

'Michael?' replied Zephaniel.

Michael spoke softly but purposefully.

'The Fallen have failed in every attempt to overcome the light. When the originators of the dark refused to show reverence to man, deciding man should serve them, we have been in conflict. We have triumphed when the shadows appeared to have been victorious.'

Michael paused, he was not sure his assumptions, his gut feelings were correct. Although he knew if they were, the kingdom was in extreme peril. He continued.

'There have been seemingly insignificant events which are now starting to give a powerful credence to the possibility we...have a sympathiser to The Fallen within the realm!'

The chamber fell silent.

Zephaniel was the first to speak.

'That, as we are all perfectly aware would be an extremely serious situation. What is the basis behind your claim?'

'We need to start viewing individual events as a whole.' Michael stood, pacing assisted his thought process. 'The slaying of a Bridge Maker may not have been predictable, an event which could have easily been missed by the Scroll Readers. But two? A duplication in a similar event would not have gone unnoticed. Whilst we may have been powerless to avert it, we should have been alerted. Events and ramifications the Scroll Readers would have had some insight into, but they did not. Then we have a protector missing. Not unusual for a small period of time, there are many reasons for a protector to disappear from our view. But we do know previously he has had a clash with a daemon, in which he himself was wounded. He recovered, returned to his entity and disappeared almost immediately.'

Michael continued to pace followed closely by the gaze of his fellow council members.

'We are yet to hear word of his fate. We do know his entity has also been the subject of some interest to Samsaweel. The Fallen have not been known to send a high status angel to the side of an entity unless behind it there is a purpose which serves their cause.'

Michael slowed his pace around the table, periods of pause were interspersed with the silence of thought from the assembled audience.

'A cause we have normally been aware of. As we know, an entities scroll contains many paths. If they choose one path it will lead them to a destiny maybe very different had they chosen to ignore it. The Scroll Readers become aware, and if necessary will notify the appropriate council. A scroll cannot be changed. But events which occur through the scrolls in which The Fallen may have the opportunity to take some advantage of, can be, to the best of our abilities, countered.'

Gadriel interrupted 'The entity, what part do they have to play in the slaying of the Bridge Makers?'

'As far as I can see Gadriel, nothing.'

Gadriel frowned.

'That is the issue. We are seemingly blind to any of the factors I believe are being laid down to distract us from The Fallen's greater plan. The entity has shown the desire to communicate through the angelic wall. He has, in the past, not been swayed by the attitudes of his world. Although rare in the current times, it is not unusual. Why would he interest the attention of an archangel though? I went to the Chamber of Scrolls to have a look at the entities' scroll. Whilst it shows potential, there was nothing within it which I believe would interest The Fallen hierarchy.'

'I am at a loss Michael to see how all these fit together, or how you can envisage an attack from within' commented Uslael.

'The danger Uslael is what we cannot see. It is the parts of the image that we are not aware of. That image is being hidden, I believe, through intent. That can only be achieved from within!'

Malach's head was spinning. Samsaweel's confession The Fallen had been responsible for the death of Cameron's mother, forced a rage within him never felt before to rise into a grip of needed revenge. Every joint and muscle groaned with pain as he attempted to sit up. He was sure if he turned round and looked at the spot on the wall he hit, his imprint would be imbedded within the hard rock. The past returned to him, he was inside Cameron's body, his pathetic frame standing over the deep hole in the earth in which his mother had just been gently lowered. Malach felt the draw of pain which flooded through every fibre of Cameron's being. The shuddered sobs welling through the very arteries that gave him life. The arteries that were part of the lifeless body which lay within the dark wooden casket. Malach tried to draw the crush of grief which restricted Cameron's breathing, but the boy had driven the grief deep within him. The protector only succeeded in wrapping his wings around the boy, a protective wall which was a futile gesture.

Why take Rebecca? What purpose does Cameron have within The Fallen? Why do they need to 'coerce' his belief? Malach put his head in his hands, nothing made any sense.

A glint of metal caught his eye.

A metallic object lay on the floor, just within the door area of the cell. Malach crawled over, he stretched out his hand but it was just out of reach. He closed his eyes and concentrated his mind, the object became the only focused subject within a void of black, but it did not move. Malach realised that his powers were rendered useless within the confines of The Fallen city.

With each flicker of light from the becketed orb the metallic object teased him. There was no way he could reach out and grab it with his hand. He lay on his front, spread his wing, the tip of his feathers groped agonisingly at the object. He managed to tease a small part of his wing underneath. With a quick flick he sent it flying into the wall next to him, landing with a chinking noise.

The touch of the brooch made the wound on his forearm tingle as he shifted it around in his palm. It was the insignia of The Fallen, the dagger glistened, it had a brighter sheen than the wings which had a frosted appearance, Malach recognised the brooch, it was one of two worn just above the hem on The Fallen's cloaks. Before Samsaweel's visit the floor was bare, the archangel would never be able to trace back it's whereabouts.

Samsaweel walked through the throng of entities, the screams and chants of the crowd annoyed him. He noticed Jetrel sitting at the top of the grandstand, laughing and clapping along with the people sitting next to him. With a flick of his wings the archangel joined him.

'What is going on? Where is the boy?' asked Samsaweel.

'He is down there playing the swordsman,' replied Jetrel pointing towards the gymnasium floor.

Samsaweel glanced down towards two white clad figures, parrying and thrusting.

'It is a competition. The boy is very good in fact.'

'Really' sneered the archangel.

A loud cheer echoed around the gym, Cameron lifted his fencing mask, and took a deep breath. Before replacing it, he wiped away the sweat running down the sides of his face with his forearm, Cameron returned to his marker.

'He may actually win. His opponent is very strong in attack but cannot counter from defence. When the boy has him on the back foot he scores every time.....'

'I am not interested in his prowess with a Rapier' snapped Samsaweel 'report!'

Jetrel gathered his thoughts.

'The boy's visions are increasing in length and strength. He still hangs a protective cloak over the vision but I am able to see more of it as time goes on. I have managed to see a small segment of the writing that appears through…..'

'Segments are of no use daemon, we need the full transcript,' interrupted Samsaweel.

Jetrel frowned.

'The pile of transcripts I briefly saw within the vision appears to be a vast piece of work. At the rate the boy sees his vision, it will take time. What is so important within the old man's writings?'

Samsaweel turned and gave Jetrel a contemptuous glare.

'That is not your concern! Your concern should be acquiring the confidence of the entity, to enable you to climb through into the vision and read the transcript, so that your curiosity will be resolved. If you have not got the ability to gain his confidence Jetrel. Then…' Samsaweel paused, glanced down towards Cameron. '…..you will be of no use to me. I will replace you with someone who can deliver. Let's just hope for your sake you do not let me down!'

Samsaweel spoke no more and vanished through the roof of the gymnasium.

Jetrel looked after him, then turned towards Cameron who was now standing on top of the podium. A wide grin present, a gold medal glistening hanging around his neck. I didn't have a chance to inform Samsaweel the entity seems to be able to see through the angelic wall he remembered, well it will have to wait for now. Although now I will have to act to 'gain the boy's confidence' once and for all.

Malach knew Lucifer would send his enforcers to despatch him at some point. The protector mused whether the dark prince would come and do it himself. A prospect Malach really did not relish. He decided he would rather die trying to escape, than to fall cowering in front of The Fallen; a prize sacrifice for their amusement. He twiddled the brooch in his fingers, the dagger was slightly longer than the tips of the wings, Malach inquisitively twisted the tip of it inside the small lock that secured his chains. It appeared to grip the mechanism but he just could not get enough purchase to unhinge the lock. He continued to twist and probe, the brooch's strength was in contrast to it's delicate look and feel. Becoming confident the dagger would hold strong, he drove the tip of it as far as it would go, with a sharp twist there was a reassuring click.

Free from his chains, Malach's initial jubilation became frustration as he felt the part of the wall that held the door. The seamless wall was hard, cold and oppressive. He grabbed an orb from it's becket, running the light along what he believed to be the edge of the doorway. Nothing. He could not make out even a hint of a crack, pacing around the cell, the room now seemed larger than it had done. Malach felt a deeper sense of urgency to break through the walls even though he knew nothing of what lay beyond the cell. What he was sure about, if escape was at all possible, he would only take a few steps before he was run through by a sword of The Fallen. He pressed his ear against the wall, it betrayed no sound from the opposite side. Beyond lay the very heart of The Fallen yet he felt no presence. The only way to get through the door would require patience then timing. The opportunity would have to be taken very carefully then swiftly.

Cameron now sat in the gymnasium changing rooms.

Whilst he had been speaking to his father, all the other contestants had changed and left. Cameron thought his father sounded tired, but he was ecstatic at hearing Cameron had won the nationals hopefully winning a place in the international team that would be going to Rome. A combined aroma of sweat and soap filled the room, he sat on the wooden bench, and briefly thought how much he would have given to have been able to make a phone call to his mother. His thoughts were distracted by a haze in the air on the bench opposite him. Cameron softly squinted, he could make out the very faint outline of Jetrel's head and what he was sure was a shoulder.

'Are you going to say something, that is if you can. Or are you going to disappear again?' Cameron asked as he started to undo the laces on his trainers.

'You have a fine poise with the sword' replied Jetrel, he did not really expect Cameron to hear him. He had never personally known any entity having heard the spoken words, let alone engage in conversation with an angel.

'Thank you....' said Cameron, 'did you see the competition?'

'Indeed.'

Cameron stopped changing out of his fencing clothing, and stared through Jetrel trying to get a clearer picture of the him.

'Who are you? Are you a ghost?' Cameron asked.

'A ghost! Not quite.' Jetrel studied the boy, his scruffy dark brown hair, lay down in sweaty clumps. His piercing deep emerald green eyes, windows into the mind of a boy far beyond his human years.

'Not quite?' questioned Cameron.

'Well...I am not a ghost in the manner your entity

teachings has you believe in the existence of spirits....'
Jetrel kept pausing trying to find the best way to explain to Cameron what he was. Something he had not actually given a great deal of thought to himself, so how was he going to explain it to an entity.

'So what are you then?' Cameron gazed at the shifting haze which distorted the row of benches behind Jetrel.

'I am a guardian, a protector, who has been assigned to accompany you through your time within the kingdom of entities.....I believe we are called angels.' Jetrel saw Cameron's expression gave away no reaction.

'Angels....so you are my angel?'

'Yes.....everyone is accompanied by them.'

Cameron got up, switched the main lights off in the gymnasium changing room. The small auxiliary lights stayed on and it took a moment for his eyes to adjust to the deep gloom. He sat back down opposite the angel. Cameron could now see the figure before him was the size of an average man, slightly smaller than his dad Cameron thought, although he was more well built. Jetrel had what Cameron had heard his mother say about certain film stars; chiselled features, he had dark hair, almost pitch black. Cameron was unsettled by the lack of any apparent colour in his eyes, but was distracted away from these by the white emblem of The Fallen which appeared to lift from the angel's breastplate.

'Really, and what do you protect us from?' Cameron spoke with a bitterness behind the words.

'That is a difficult question, protect is a misleading word. Guide, would be a better choice. There are many choices you will encounter during your life within this realm. Choices that will be based upon your held knowledge,

knowledge yet to be gained, your inner perception, inner strength. Choices which will require decisions based upon a hidden cloak, that hidden cloak is the main reason for our presence.'

'I don't understand' said Cameron.

'You are young....'

Cameron sighed.

'...it is the experiences you gain as you grow which will, but not always, bring understanding. I am here to guide you against the forces who would want to take advantage, of your, how shall I say, qualities.'

Cameron frowned at the angel's praise.

'Qualities, what qualities?'

'Well how many people do you know, can see and converse with an angel?'

Cameron thought about it. He was certain there were far more than just one! The question should be he thought, how many would admit to it?

'I can't see any wings, if you are an angel, and not a ghost you would have wings.'

Jetrel stood. Cameron saw the dark angel's cloak fall and settle behind him, his powerful wings spread and with a flick, a wave of cool air wafted over Cameron. Cameron gazed in awe. Jetrel saw some emotion within the boy for the first time.

'Now is there anything else you would like to see, for me to prove I am not a spirit?' Jetrel asked.

Cameron shook his head.

'Good!'

Cameron grabbed a towel from his bag, he buried his face into it wiping away the sweat that collected on his forehead, and ran down into his eyes. It also gave him an opportunity to collect his thoughts. He had been prepared to confront the angel at some point, but this moment seemed extremely surreal. Maybe the angel would not be there when he put the towel down, he peeked, the angel was still there.

'Are you always with me?' asked Cameron.

'Not always, I know when to be discreet. I am with you all the time my presence may be needed.'

'When I am not in need of your presence, what do you do then?' asked Cameron.

'Amuse myself.'

Cameron furrowed his brow, but did not feel the need to find out how an angel 'amused himself' at the moment. Cameron felt unsure about the presence in front of him. Whilst not feeling threatened or in any danger at all, an inner sense made him feel slightly uncomfortable. He decided it would be wise to keep this all at arms length, for now at least. He would also keep the contact with the angel to himself. No one needed to know, just yet.

'I need to have a shower and get changed. I have to meet my friend soon.'

'Of course....' replied Jetrel with a small bow of his head '.....as I have said, I know how to be discreet, you need not worry about telling me your intentions. I have done alright up to now. I have welcomed our conversation.'

Jetrel stood and moved towards the changing room door.

'Oh before you go. What is your name?' called Cameron.

Jetrel stopped, he turned and faced Cameron with a smile.

'Malach, my name is Malach!'

Chapter Fourteen

Michael pondered upon the order given by Zephaniel. To seek a traitor within the Enlightened would not be an easy task. If his assumptions were correct and a collaborator of The Fallen sat amongst them, they had so far been discreet enough to avoid rousing any suspicions. Michael knew assigning an archangel or any other high ranking angel would attract too much attention. The kingdom was a vast metropolis which served the world of man, a vast metropolis where nothing went unnoticed. Discretion was paramount.

'I have another request Zahabriel.'

Michael looked at his cavalry commander, the archangel could see the crucifixion of Harial had affected the experienced officer greatly. Outwardly he had continued in his self assured duties, betraying the inward torment that gripped him. Zahabriel was blaming the loss of his cavalry trooper on himself. Michael sensed the inner guilt. A distraction was needed, a double edged sword which would serve two purposes. Zahabriel would be assigned on Michael's new task, kept busy. He would be senior enough to carry the orders of the archangel but not senior enough, Michael hoped, to draw attention to himself.

Zahabriel puzzled over the information Michael had given him. He knew the archangel was serious, but he could not bring himself to believe within the realm lay a traitor.

'Are you sure Sire?' asked Zahabriel with an air of incredulity.

Michael was not surprised at Zahabriel questioning the assumption. Michael, after all, knew that is all it was, for now.

'Events which have led to The Fallen being camped within the Forest of Wandering Spirits, leads me to believe some assistance has been given. That assistance....' said Michael with a hiss, 'has to be emanating from within. We have a protector missing, we have not heard anything about his fate or whereabouts for some time now. The interesting aspect to this is he is the protector of a young entity who has acquired the interest of a fallen archangel... Samsaweel!'

Zahabriel raised his eyebrows, 'well, well....Samsaweel.'

'For now commander that is all the information I can give you. I want you to visit the Chamber of Scrolls. Discreetly seek out any unusual activity, any behaviour that has occurred, which in the first instant would seem innocuous, but may provide a link to my assumptions. Unfortunately it is the only guidance I can give at this stage, the rest is down to you. I repeat Zahabriel, discretion is paramount. I need to know whether we have an enemy within. If they become aware they have roused our suspicions they will go underground, making our task impossible. To give you a symbol of authority to bypass any obstacles which may confront a cavalry commander.....' Michael said with a smile, '....would raise whispers, you need to work with your initiative. This contains all the information you will require at this stage to begin with.'

Zahabriel took the crystal tablet, he read the names of

the protector and entity, names which were unfamiliar.

'Anything else Sire?'

Michael shook his head, Zahabriel bowed and left the archangel with his thoughts.

Dagon brushed his finger along the wall of the hologram image of the Enlightened city. The holographic map of the vast kingdom shimmered before Bernael, Ertrael and Beleth who sat around the table watching the city wall distort in a soft wave.

'I believe it is time to formerly announce our presence to our….how shall we say….not so accommodating hosts.' Dagon continued to probe individual buildings with his finger.

'Excellent, the Core has started to become restless' cried Bernael, 'they will welcome the distraction from inactivity.'

Dagon greeted his cavalry captain with a steely gaze. 'If inactivity is a problem with the cavalry Bernael, maybe they would appreciate being the vanguard of our attack!'

Bernael did not respond to the stern rebuke from Dagon. He had been held responsible for the break through of their camp lines by the unicorn trooper, he knew it would be foolish to displease his commander further.

'What is the plan?' asked Beleth

'Our orders are quite explicit….' replied Dagon, '… we stay within the realm, and probe, occupy their forces, distract them from our quest within the world of entities. We do not however, attack in force. We do not want to commit ourselves to a full scale battle with the Enlightened…. yet!'

'Would it not be unwise to attack with a force large

enough to impact on their strength?' Asked Ertrael 'a token number committed would be easily repelled, increasing their resolve.'

Dagon agreed, probing the Enlightened may well bring about heavy loses. The result would strengthen their morale, but he again reminded his assembled commanders of their purpose. Distraction .

'My plan is to attack here….' Dagon pointed to a section of the wall to the west of the Gate of Arabah, '…..Beleth we will probe with your siege engines and Bernael's cavalry. I believe this is the weakest section. It is the furthest point from their garrison. Their city buildings lie beyond this section of wall, projectiles sent over the wall will cause chaos. Projectiles into the wall will over time weaken it. Any opportunity in the future to exploit this weakness will lead us to capitalise and send in the Core and the Wolves.'

'The winged troopers may well suffer a high rate of casualties if sent in before their forces on the wall are neutralised, or at best occupied,' stated Bernael.

'Better they die in glory than boredom!' quipped Dagon.

Zahabriel peered across the gentle waves of the Sea of Souls towards the jetty, the seven palaces fell away in the distance. Their presence magnificent even at the far edge of the huge sea. The thought of a traitor troubled him greatly, he was a soldier of the light, he had witnessed death and pain in it's rawest form. He had felt the breath of his enemy on his face, the fading to grey of their sable eyes as he drew his sword from their chest. He had held his comrades in his arms, the light ebbing from them as their courage and honour stemmed their cries of pain. The death of Harial had reached the core of all he held decent, he knew The Fallen to be merciless adversaries, but to crucify his trooper. The cavalry commander chilled at the thought of his troopers left behind in the clearing within the Forest of Wandering Spirits; these deaths at the hand of a traitor.

Zahabriel walked up the white granite steps which led up to the entrance of the Chamber of Scrolls. He passed between two of the four pillars supporting the cherub decorated architrave and frieze, he pushed the two massive granite doors firmly which opened very easily, belying their huge individual weight. Walking into the cool surroundings of the cavernous marbled hall, he was surprised at the inactivity which permeated through the great hall. A small clerk in the centre of the hall sat in the middle of a circular counter in the centre of the floor. As Zahabriel walked towards him, his footsteps echoed loudly making him feel uncomfortable and clumsy. The cavalry commander had left his uniform behind, his armour would certainly have drawn far more attention than his simple tunic and skirt, although the gold hem on the sleeves and skirt and the gold tip of his wings would certainly give away the fact he was a member of the Powers to a keen eye.

'Can I help?' asked the clerk, warmly greeting Zahabriel with a big smile.

'I would like to see a scroll if that is possible?' Zahabriel asked.

'Of course' the clerk hauled onto the side of his counter a great bound book of parchment, each page contained a list of infinite names and corresponding scroll numbers. 'Now then, it would help if you know the key number for the said entity, if not do not worry, it will just take us a moment longer to trace their scroll. Now then let me see.' The clerk read the crystal tablet Zahabriel held up in front of him, then dragged his finger down the seemingly endless list of names. 'Ah here we are....' the clerk wrote down the key number '...there that is the number you need. The scroll will be found within the fifth room over to the left, you will... what is that?'

The clerk was interrupted by the sound of war horns.

'War horns of The Fallen!' cried Zahabriel, he turned and ran from the hall.

Zahabriel reached the steps to the west side of the front wall just has a projectile of flame fired from The Fallen's massive Chetuber siege engines struck. As it hit the bottom of the wall the flaming missile sent a white hot tumult up it's side, the troops on the palisade turned away, covering their heads with their shields as the flames licked over the wall edge. Two more missiles struck as Zahabriel clambered to the top of the steps, all around him troops cowered and scurried away on all fours.

'Stand to!' Zahabriel bellowed.

The soldiers froze, before them the cavalry commander appeared, he presented almost naked to the troops who were unaccustomed to seeing Zahabriel without his armour. He reached out and grabbed the nearest trooper by his back plate, hauling him to his feet.

'Go get me some armour and a sword, and be quick about it trooper!'

The soldier nodded, now was not the time to point out to the commander he was not a trooper as he stumbled down the steps as he hurried away.

Zahabriel turned towards a roar above his head, he was

covered in a rush of hot air as a Chetuber projectile hurtled towards him. He threw himself down, just in time as the projectile clipped the walled parapet. It's trajectory abruptly changed as Zahabriel and the troopers within his vicinity were showered with hot sparks. The ball of destruction bounced like a pebble skimming across a pond, with a deafening roar it leaped over the two inner walls and smashed into the houses beyond. Fire spread rapidly, Zahabriel knelt, frantically looking around him searching the air for further missiles.

Projectiles continued to smash into the same section of the wall. Zahabriel wondered how much punishment the wall could take before it began to falter.

'Move away from this section!' he cried gesturing towards the prone bodies of the soldiers seeking as much cover as they could behind the parapet.

He moved away from the targeted section. Just as he peered over the wall out towards the forest, a breathless soldier arrived by his side carrying a set of armour and a sword.

'Excellent....' Zahabriel frantically put the armour on '....now wait with me. I need to see what is going on.'

He tightened the helmet strap, gripping the helmet between his hands he wriggled it until it felt comfortable. Zahabriel could see a row of four Chetubers in the distance just in front of the tree line. Either side of them were single Arogen catapults. To the left of the siege engines he was drawn to some movement from the trees; a black mass moved slowly as one then spread like a swarm of flies.

Zahabriel turned to the soldier.

'Run to the east wall, there are winged cavalry on their way, make sure the officers over there have seen them. Tell them to concentrate the fire of the ballista and archers at them. They must not get over into the city! Then return to me. Go!'

Zahabriel watched the soldier disappear down the steps. Another roar from above made him swirl round, this time he was not quick enough. A projectile smashed into the top of the parapet. He was knocked to the side as a surge of white hot air hit him. Two soldiers beside him screamed, they clawed the air as their bodies became engulfed in flame. One of the soldiers veered off of the wall, falling away over the parapet, his screams dying away as he fell. The other continued his death march towards Zahabriel, he stared in horror as the soldier's screams were now drowned out by the roar of flame. His flapping arms, breaking off small dancing balls of fire. The soldier stalled and fell to the ground next to Zahabriel with a heavy thud, the tips of the flames scorching Zahabriel's legs. The unicorn commander scrambled backwards, kicking the dead soldier off of the wall. He disappeared leaving a smoky trail rising upward.

Zahabriel try to stand, he winced as the skin down his left side which had been exposed to the blast and the flaming soldier, smarted. He crouched on one bended knee, gathering his thoughts, his attention drawn to the black mass rapidly approaching the east wall. The projectiles continued to batter the west wall, a few entered the residential area; the carnage awesome. Everything within the impact zone, buildings, angels had been incinerated, around the perimeters of the craters lay the shattered remains of broken bodies. Zahabriel focused his thoughts to the forces outside the wall, he could not see any immediate danger to the west wall, apart from the siege engines.

'Troopers to the east wall, now! Prepare to repel attack from the winged cavalry!' Zahabriel cried as he ran to the east wall. He jumped over the torn carcasses of several soldiers. The boiling mass rose high into the sky, it then swooped racing down directly towards the east wall.

'Archers! Ballistae!' cried the officers of the Powers, the orders rippling along the wall.

Zahabriel ran across the section of wall over the arch of the Gates of Arabah as a cloud of arrows fired into the oncoming mass of Fallen winged cavalry. The front ranks faltered as the volley struck, though their weight of numbers pushed onwards as The Fallen cavalry hit by the first fusillade fell to the ground. Zahabriel's progress was barred by the massed ranks of soldiers on the east wall, he looked across to the west side where The Fallen's siege machines continued to pound the wall. Thick black smoke swirled skywards from the fires which were spreading within the residential area. The unicorn commander glanced back round as frantic orders were relayed along the east wall as further volleys flew into the front ranks of the oncoming cavalry.

'Shields!'

Zahabriel looked on as the first volley of arrows from The Fallen cavalry rained down. A soldier within the rear rank twisted, falling from the wall as an arrow cut deep into his shoulder. Zahabriel pressed into the mass, crouching behind the protective wall of shields, just behind him a soldier fell to his knees as an arrow penetrated just under the cheek piece of his helmet. The soldier was frozen by his screams as the pain drove through his body. Zahabriel grabbed the shoulder strap of the soldier's breast plate as the soldier started to fall backwards, his momentum taking him over the edge of the wall. Zahabriel was slammed into the floor of the wall as his arm bore the full weight of the stricken soldier. The cavalry commander grimaced as with all his strength he tried to pull the soldier back up, his arm muscles began to burn, his fingers began to slide from underneath the leather hilt.

'Grab my arm!' he cried, 'Soldier! Grab my arm!'

The soldier did not hear Zahabriel's order, he was staring into the sky, screams driving from his body.

'Grab my arm........I can't hold....'

Zahabriel's grip slipped from the soldier's armour, the soldier seemed to hang in mid air for a split moment then with a jerk fell away. He watched the soldier's journey until he hit the ground.

All around him, everything moved in a slow silence. The noise of battle lingered in drawn out cries. He was brought back to the realness of the moment as several soldiers jolted him as they ran past, back toward the Gate of Arabah. Zahabriel stood, he could see a group of approximately thirty dark angels had broken from the flying units and were now engaged in hand to hand combat on the wall.

Running back Zahabriel struggled to get near to the action as the parapet was choked with soldiers pressing towards the separate mini battle upon the main gate.

The isolated group of Fallen angels had disobeyed orders, their comrades now aware, circled and supported them by firing arrows into the ever growing body of Enlightened troops pressing towards them. Zahabriel picked up a shield discarded by it's owner who had no future use of it, two arrows protruding from the side of his torso saw to that.

The group of dark angels had formed a circle, their small

cavalry shields forming an inadequate barrier, but in experienced hands were proving a stubborn obstacle. Their short swords were very effective in close combat, as the rear ranks of Powers pressed the massed ranks of the Enlightened forward in their eagerness to expel the Fallen from the city walls, it became increasingly difficult for the Enlightened troops to penetrate with any potency with their longer swords. In such close personal confines the majority had discarded their spears as the press forced them closer into the grip of battle.

The small group of winged cavalry had started to inflict heavy casualties on the front ranks of Enlightened troops. The bodies cut down were now beginning to thwart any attempt to break through amongst a determined enemy, Zahabriel was gradually getting closer to the frontline. He pressed through the gaps that were slowly appearing. He knew the circle had to be broken, to break through amongst them would give them the advantage of numbers and space to use their longer swords more effectively. He was three rows back from the maelstrom, he kept urging the soldiers to try to retreat a little to give them the space they needed to engage with a little more effectiveness.

Out of the corner of his eye he caught a glimpse of an object falling from the sky. Turning quickly he saw that it was a dark angel struck through the chest by a ballista bolt. Before he could cry out a warning the angel crashed into the troops in front of him. Two angels on the edge of the wall were carried away over it, the row of angels in front were thrown forward into the shield wall of The Fallen. Zahabriel saw one of the dark angels thrust his short sword deep into the face of a prostrate soldier. Another was almost sliced through as a short sword was brought down between his neck and shoulder, the light extinguished without a cry.

'Hold!' the unicorn commander bellowed.

Zahabriel was now in front of the pressing mass. He lifted his sword high into the air, took another deep breath and ordered the Enlightened troops to hold their position.

'On me! Form a shield wall on me!' he cried.

The Powers drew in line with the unicorn commander, their long shields joined as one articulating barrier. They were now ten paces away from the shield wall of The Fallen. Zahabriel could see that the opposite side of the circle was also engaged in heavy fighting.

The cavalry commander kissed the point of his sword where the blade entered the hilt and whispered 'deliver me from the lion's mouth, and my lowliness by the horns of unicorns.'

Zahabriel lifted his sword high into the air. Looking along the line he could see the soldiers awaited his command.

'On me.....forward!' he cried.

The improvised wall moved forward. Part of the line faltered as they clambered over the bodies laying in small heaps. Zahabriel focused on the dark angel directly in front of him, his black eyes penetrating through the cheek pieces of his helmet. Behind him he heard several screams as another volley of arrows from the circling wing cavalry rained down.

'Steady! Steady!' Zahabriel cried as looked along the line.

The lines of Enlightened let out a war cry and jumped forward into the enemy line. The dark angel opposite Zahabriel jerked forward trying to close the gap even further, he thrust his short sword at Zahabriel's head. The unicorn commander twisted to the side, the dark angel's lunge fell short. As Zahabriel twisted back he swung his longer and heavier sword down, the dark angel brought his shield up just in time to block the blow. The power of Zahabriel's attack knocked the angel's shield arm back into his midriff, he lost his balance and stepped backwards. Zahabriel saw the opportunity and threw himself forward into the dark angel, pushing him further back into the centre of the circle creating the gap he needed.

Zahabriel did not give the angel time to recover, he swung is sword high at his head then low to each side of the dark angel's chest. The angel frantically parried each attack with his shield, in desperation the Fallen angel lunged at the unicorn commander. Zahabriel danced away from the thrust, as his adversary passed with all his strength he swung his sword bringing the blade down on the back of his neck. The blow and his momentum carried the Sable Core soldier into the back of a dark angel throwing him forward onto the sword of an Enlightened soldier.

The circle now gave way. The Powers surged forward; the surviving angels of the winged cavalry realising that the situation was now lost, thrust themselves into the air. They disappeared for a brief moment over the parapet, swooped and climbed, joining the legions still probing the east wall.

As they did so, in the distance the sound of a war horn drifted across the plains. The projectiles from the siege engines ceased, the winged legions retreated back beyond the tree line of The Forest of Wandering Spirits.

Zahabriel stood tall upon the wall, his chest heaving as he sucked in large volumes of air, every muscle and sinew tightening in protest. At his feet lay the bodies of several

Fallen Sable Core, their bodies entwined with those of Enlightened troops. Numerous projectiles had carried over the walls landing within the city itself, causing immense devastation to buildings and life. He looked across towards the residential sector which was now a vast cauldron, black smoke billowed skyward blocking out part of the cavalry commander's view of the city.

Cries from officers brought those soldiers on the wall who had survived the assault to attention, orders barked out, the clearing up process began immediately. Zahabriel gazed out across towards the forest far in the distance, the Fallen had probed a section of the wall, an assault that served no other purpose than to send a stark message to the Enlightened; they were not here just to sightsee! He shook his head in dismay, to think that this could be the responsibility of an informer….a traitor! Zahabriel strode back through the city. The concept of an angel within the walls, ready to betray, stung his mind into a fog of disbelief. The consequence of that betrayal was the smell of destruction and death that now dug at his senses. His steps lengthened, his pace quickened towards the Chamber of Scrolls. Each stride rejuvenated his strength, a determination grew deep inside him knowing that if Michael's suspicions were correct, time may not be on their side. He pondered over the depth of treachery, he had heard the whispers that had filtered throughout the kingdom following the slaying of the Bridge-Makers. He had decided to allow others to sit around the fountains and pontificate over the cause and reason, knowing the destiny of action would always be revealed in the end. He know wondered whether there was a connection, the whispers in his mind grew in volume.

Chapter Fifteen

The wooden bench sat on a knoll overlooking Crawford Lake. During the winter it was an exposed place, the wood was split, and had the dull grey appearance through being battered by the elements. Cameron's face tingled with the soft warm spring winds which brushed gentle ripples on the lake and travelled over the knoll, finding a hiding place within the dark wood behind. Cameron looked at his new companion with a cautious stare, he had kept a distance from the daemon since talking to him after the fencing competition. Cameron had acknowledged his presence when the opportunity presented itself, always wary about the impact it would have on his friends if he were seen talking into thin air. He felt a sense of being, not felt since he had been dropped off at Byford by the stand in driver, whose name at this moment in time escaped him. The feeling he thought was similar but different, although he could not explain to himself what the difference was exactly. Cameron could not put his finger on what it was, although it was enough for him to decide that he would tread cautiously until he was sure about what was happening.

The low spring sun made Cameron squint as he watched the faint outline of Jetrel wandering amongst the deep grass at the bottom of the knoll. A Heron sprang from the long reeds at the edge of the lake, it's large wings pumped the air as it hung in a picture frame of motionlessness, then ungraciously turned towards the marshes on the far side of the lake. A prize wriggled in it's long beak.

'So are you from heaven then?' Cameron shouted.

'Heaven?' Jetrel replied. Realising he should be, he nodded, 'yes I am from heaven.'

'What is it like?'

Jetrel had never been to the angel kingdom, and the only tales he had heard about it were from the words of old soldiers who had fought during the great battles of Zo-Har. He thought, paced a little more, and tried to create an image of the Enlightened city in his mind. He looked up at Cameron sitting on the bench, what am I doing he thought the boy had never been to heaven either, it is hardly a trick question, make it up, so it sounds great and full of light!

'Well, the kingdom is vast. A city of pure white, a city which is covered by light and song. Although to many it is what you want it to be.'

He knew this was a popular belief of man, to those that sought the need for heaven to exist. Heaven was a figment of need, it inhabits man's conscience where he builds a realm that encapsulates his need and belief.

'For many it serves a purpose for them to have an image which maybe very personal rather than coldly factual.'

'So you are saying heaven is an actual place, a city like London say. Rather than an infinite space where people go' Cameron asked frowning quizzically.

'Heaven is an actual place. That is probably as much as the similarity with your London lays.' Jetrel struggled to find the right words to explain to Cameron, he was very aware that the boy's perception may well search further beyond his ability to see an angelic companion.

'So what part of heaven are you from?' Cameron asked

coldly which did not go a miss with Jetrel.

'Erm... I am from the... angel city. Yes the angel city, that is where I am from.' Jetrel scratched the side of his head nervously. 'It is a part of the kingdom where we all live, when we are not busy roaming the kingdom of entities.'

'Entities being us?'

'Yes.'

'So what do you do then, why are you always with me?' Cameron gesticulated his hand in a frantic wave in front of his face, the spring winds had roused an inquisitive bumble bee. Too inquisitive for Cameron's liking.

'Well, as I have said, I am your protector. I am here to guide you, help you make the right decisions which will assist you in fulfilling your role within this realm. It is a thankless task!' Jetrel peered up towards Cameron.

'Thankless!' Cameron snapped 'What have I to be thankful for?'

'Well....let me put some definition on that statement. It was not pointed at you, rather a generalised statement of angelic opinion directed towards entities as a whole. Every entity emerges into their world with the ability to seek communication with their protector. The vast majority lose it through the influences they are exposed to as they travel through their years. Some even dismiss the existence of angels altogether, yet we remain loyal and by the side of every single entity. We whisper the words of direction, yet we are never acknowledged.'

Cameron stared across towards the far banks of Crawford Lake, he shivered gently as a fresh breeze, slightly cooler than the ones before chilled the exposed skin on his arms and neck. 'Why do you call yourselves protectors?' he asked.

'There are many things which lay within your realm and those beyond, that would, how shall we say? Re-direct your energies, for a purpose that would benefit them rather than you. Depending on how receptive the entity is, we aim to protect them, and guide them onto the path that will fulfill their destiny.'

'What happens if someone does not fulfill their destiny? What happens if someone dies before they have done it?' asked Cameron.

Jetrel thought about how to answer Cameron's question. He turned away and glared hard into the spring sun. How would a protector answer that? he thought.

'Everyone fulfils their destiny…..there is a purpose for everyone, the success of the journey is discovering what that purpose is whilst they tread within this realm. Or for the ones left behind, to find the reason behind what may seem a quick passing.' Jetrel smiled, he was impressed with that explanation himself. He watched Cameron as his words mulled throughout the entities' mind.

'Cam! Cam!'

Cameron and Jetrel turned, running down the pathway was Josh holding aloft a piece of paper. He stumbled, regained his footing then took a small jump over an overgrown bramble straddling the winding pathway.

'Cam!' he breathlessly shouted.

Before Cameron could reply Josh was at the top of the knoll standing beside him, he struggled to speak as the words were swallowed up by hard gasps of air.

'Cam, look… you've… done it!' said Josh doubled over, holding the piece of paper high at arms length flapping in the breeze.

Cameron grabbed the paper from Josh's hand, he

quickly scanned through seeing his confirmation at being selected for the national fencing team to represent Great Britain had arrived.

'Wow! Yes!' Cameron cried with a jubilant clenched fist. Cameron slapped Josh's back. 'Thanks for bringing it down here Josh.'

'That's ok....I couldn't find you, it took me ages!' Josh stood up and looked about him noting that his friend was alone. 'What are you doing down here anyway?' Josh asked looking around inquisitively.

'Not a lot, just having a bit of time to myself.' Cameron glanced back down the knoll, the long grass where Jetrel had been swayed vigorously as the spring winds increased with the setting evening sun.

The four walls of his cell begun to close around him as Malach became ever more frustrated in his captivity. He had scanned every inch of the walls that held him captive for an opening, an opportunity to make a bid for freedom. A bid which Malach knew would be nothing more than a defiant gesture, he had felt every contour of the section of wall that held the doorway. Not even a hairline crack gave away any hint of an opening. The protector had to be very careful with the amount of time he paced around his cell, free from his shackles the walls gave away no trace of any sounds that would warn him of someone entering the room.

He returned back to the wall where the chains were attached, sat down and clipped the metal rings around his ankles. He wondered what lay beyond the doorway, where within The Fallen city was he? Was he actually in the city? How closely guarded was he? He knew there was at least one guard on the other side of the wall, he had seen the figure standing there when someone came through. Any escape bid would inevitably mean he would have to deal with at least two dark angels. Any more than two, then any slim hope of success would be instantly reduced to a suicidal attempt. Malach had decided an escape bid would have to be initiated with as many factors in his favour at the moment he made his move. The most important factor would be surprise. His attack would have to be swift, and merciless.

Malach needed information. His captors were, despite the guard outside the cell, confident that the chances of the protector escaping from his cell, let alone the actual city, plus the thought he would actually attempt an escape bid, were non existent. Malach decided he would lull The Fallen deeper into their sense of security, a position which may give him an advantage rather than them. He needed to probe one of his regular visitors. Not Lucifer! It would be far too dangerous, the dark prince would immediately see through the ploy. The smaller shifty dark angel that occasionally accompanied Lucifer, was never a lone visitor, or for that matter much of a communicator. The snap of light from the becketed orbs interrupted his thoughts, he stretched his legs out, resting his back on the wall. One of the clips on an ankle lock slipped apart causing the metal collar to fall to the ground with a loud metallic clank. Malach shook his head disconcertedly, if it had happened in the presence of a dark angel all would have been lost. He stretched his hand behind him and ran it underneath his wing, feeling for a strand of hair which grew by the knuckle. He wound the plucked strand of hair around the bracket, waggling it he was sure it was just strong enough to hold the lock together, but weak enough to snap when

Malach needed to move quickly. He returned to his thoughts. The 'ferrety' angel is an unknown quantity. The only angel arrogant enough to gloat at my dire predicament, possibly giving away freely the information I need to know about city beyond to at least give me some chance, would be Samsaweel!

Chapter Sixteen

Malach held the image he had in his mind of the layout of the Fallen city. He had managed to carefully sift the information from his conversations with, mainly Samsaweel, although the protector had sought out opportunities to question any visitor he had about the immediate geography beyond the cell door. Lucifer, Malach noted, had been conspicuous by his absence and had not returned since leaving in a veil of fury. His impression of the city was a maze of corridors, it appeared that sections of the city branched off of these corridors into large pantheons. He had gained a vital piece of information when the dark archangel had let out that each corridor ultimately led into the great hall, from this hall, through it's large main doors was the route out of the city. Malach had been right to assume the dark angels were arrogant enough to speak freely about the city. Even so his attempt would only be a futile one, ultimately stemmed by an honourable death. The moment he made his move he knew the consequences would be severe. He sat back against the wall of his cell, at least he hoped it would be swift. The protector knew how and when he would strike, after that point it would all be down to luck.

It had been quite a while since Samsaweel had taken it upon himself to pay the Fallen's guest a visit. The conversations between the two had grown into deeper interchanges of dialogue, mainly through the veiled deceit of the protector. Malach glared at Samsaweel as he leant against the far wall, the flickering orbs either side of him made his face contort in shifting shapes of shadow.

'I have no idea what Lucifer has planned for you?' Samsaweel said, each word being laughed out. 'Admittedly it does not look good. It would appear he has grown tired of you. The novelty has worn off so to speak.'

'Quite! For me the novelty wore off a long, long time ago.' Malach replied 'still, when I return to the Enlightened city I can safely say I will look back on my time here, without any fondness or regard whatsoever.'

Samsaweel let out a burst of laughter. He walked to the section of the wall in which the door began to appear, the hardness of the surface appeared to melt as if an ice wall had been subjected to the white rays of the sun. He lowered his voice.

'I should not waste your time with such pointless dreams protector. Your city will shortly be only fit to receive the scavenging souls of the lost.' Samsaweel turned and made to step through the doorway.

Malach launched himself forward with a loud guttural cry, the shackles fell away with a loud metallic clank. Samsaweel jerked round, his body frozen, stunned at the brief sight of the protector surging at him. Free of his chains. Malach hit the dark archangel with as much strength as he could muster. The force threw Samsaweel through the door his body locked in Malach's savage grip. As the two angels fell through the doorway into the corridor they clipped the guard standing outside, the force coupled with the element of surprise sent him sprawling. Malach and Samsaweel crashed headlong into the far wall of the corridor. The protector heard a sickening thwack and now lay on top of Samsaweel who was a lifeless deadweight. He frantically jerked his arms free from under the body of the dark angel as he heard a groan come from the guard who was laying prostrate against the wall. Malach saw the guard had obviously been dazed, he was gently shaking his head, he knew the guard had to be silenced immediately; a cry for help and all would be lost. He pulled Samsaweel's body over, grabbed his sword, a sharp burning sensation drove deep through the scar on his arm, with a grimace he pulled the sword from the dark angel's scabbard.

The guard shakily got himself to his knees, he glanced around confused, then with a sharp intake of air his chest was driven through with Samsaweel's sword. He fell back against the wall, Malach stared deep into his black eyes, he could actually see the deep shock and surprise that ran through the guard as he stared up at the protector standing over him. Malach let go of the sword and stepped back, his deep breaths echoed down through the corridor. The guard grunted, Malach was shocked to see his hand feel for the hilt of the sword. He took another step backward, freezing for a moment paralysed by dread as he realised that he had used a Sabled sword on a Fallen angel. A sword that could only strike the light from an Enlightened angel, whilst it had given him vital seconds, it would not kill him.

A swell of anger surged through him. He would not return to the cell, if he was to die, he would die fighting. He grabbed the guard's shield. The dark angel had propped himself back up onto his knees, and was tentatively pulling the sword from his chest. Malach swung the shield high above his head, he tightened his muscles, and drove the side of the heavy shield into the side of the guard's head. The dark angel slumped heavily to the ground, his helmet bounced along the corridor.

Malach dropped the shield and fell into a crouch using the corridor wall to support him. His chest heaved, his arms and legs began to burn with the exertion. He stared at the lifeless bodies of the two dark angels, sure the commotion would have been heard. He peered down the long corridor which turned in a large arc, then turned and glanced down the opposite part of the corridor which also ran away in a long arc, nothing. Malach tensed, he expected to hear the ominous signs of heavy footsteps as legions of the Sable Core ran to cut him down. Stepping softly along the wall, he reached the beginning of the arc in the corridor, he leant craning his neck to see around the corner. His caution and fear got the better of him, he backed away. He clenched his fists in frustration, knowing he would not stand a chance of getting through the city without being seen.

The door to his cell had remained open, the tip of Samsaweel's foot was just penetrating the doorway stopping the door from closing. He grabbed the archangel's foot and pulled him half way through the doorway. The guard was a different matter, Malach grabbed him under his arms, his massive frame was a dead weight, Malach jerked the body back in short spurts. Once through into the cell Malach looked down at the large angel, he blew out his cheeks knowing that if the dark angel had managed to stand and face him one to one then the chances of him cutting him down would have been impossible.

Malach stripped the Sable guard, every part of the uniform was evidently too big. The cleaves scrapped his knees, the chest armour hung loosely, he had pulled the straps as taut as he could and still the breastplate sat in an ill-fitted manner. The cloak he clipped to the shoulder bridges of the breastplate, wafting it from side to side he noticed the awkwardness of it's hang. The hem practically brushed the floor. He looked over the helmet twisting it in his hands, the side of it had a large indent where he had slammed the side of the shield into it. Luckily the helmet was too big for his head so the indent just scraped the side of his scalp, just above his ear. With the long white plume the helmet felt very heavy on his head, the plume pulled it backward, then sideways as he moved his head. Malach stepped through the doorway, placed the shield and spear against the corridor wall, he pushed the lower half of Samsaweel back through into the cell. He jumped back as the doorway began to solidify into the unbroken wall. The only way now was to go forward.

As Malach stepped around the arc in the corridor, he could see it continued as far as he could see. Becketed orbs at evenly spaced intervals caused shadows to flicker in blocks. He started to slowly walk towards the small square of light in the distance. Slowly at first, then his pace quickened as he felt a surge to get to the end of the corridor as soon as possible. He checked himself, knowing that it would not have to take a keen eye to notice the conspicuous smallest member of the Sable Core, let alone one that was running through the city in a uniform that would have graced an angel who had a very long spell of ill health. He looked back trying to judge how far he had walked down the corridor. It appeared he had come approximately half way. Just in front of him to his left, were two large elaborately carved doors which were closed, he did not linger to find out what was behind them, knowing that at any moment the door could open, and his bid for freedom over.

The small square of light he saw in the distance was now an open doorway which he could see led into a small hall; opposite, the corridor seemed to carry on. He leant into the hall, it was empty. On all four sides of the small hall there were corridors leading off. From the descriptions of the city gained from Samsaweel, Malach knew this was obviously a junction which branched off to other areas of the Fallen city. When he was sure he could not hear anyone approaching, he stepped into the hall, wondering which direction he should go. Remembering every corridor led to the great chamber he decided to carry straight on. This corridor was exactly the same as the last, lined orbs lit the route, although the further he walked Malach noticed the corridor started to increase in size, both in width and height.

The protector froze, ahead came the sound of voices coming from somewhere off of the corridor. His mind started to swirl, should he go back? The voices became louder, before he could turn to go back or continue onwards two small angels stepped into the corridor and walked towards him. They were two old angels, 'ferrety' he thought like the one that accompanied Lucifer. They were engrossed in conversation, and had not seen Malach in front of them. They continued to scurry towards him, their voices raised as if involved in an argument. Malach fought his most primal urge to turn and flee.

'Run where?' he muttered, his tension getting the better of his self control, the words released carried down the corridor towards the oncoming angels.

They looked up.

Malach stood paralysed in their stare. The corridor was a lot brighter than the one in which his cell was situated, but still gloomy enough for his eyes to appear black through the cheek pieces of his helmet. Malach frowned in surprise as the two angels bowed and parted, clearing the Sable Core soldier's way. Malach took a deep breath, pushing his chest out attempting to look the part. He held the shield close to him trying to hide from view his ill-fitting uniform. As he passed they did not meet his stare, then they scurried on their way without turning back. No suspicions had been roused. Malach passed by the chamber from where the two dark angels came from. One of the doors was closed, the other was half ajar. He peeked through as he passed, inside he saw a small fountain. The trickle of water brought back memories of the large fountains in the square of the angel city, past the fountain he could see a walkway which seemed to wander down towards what Malach thought was a wood. Malach could not quite make out the exact details, even though his curiosity had been pricked he did not linger. Carrying on down the corridor he passed two more chambers, their doors were closed, no noise gave away the presence of life. Malach was surprised at the quietness of the city, he had expected to have been confronted with a throng of activity at every turn. Ahead he could see another square of light at the end of the corridor, was this the great chamber or another junction hall? he thought.

Suddenly behind him a door opened, he quickened his pace.

'You! Halt!' snapped a voice behind him.

Malach came to a sharp standstill.

'Where are you going? What is your duty?'

Malach kept looking ahead, he had no desire to see who the owner of the voice was. Every fibre of his being tensed, became a coiled spring that would launch him down the corridor. He fought against the urge, knowing he would be cut down immediately.

'I....I am to report to the great conduit' Malach remembered this was what Samsaweel had called the entrance to The Fallen city during one of their conversations.

'What are you doing over here then?'

Malach could hear the voice slowly walk down the corridor towards him. Any moment now his true identity would be discovered. His quest for freedom over.

'I was escorting the archangel Samsaweel to... to the cell of the captive protector. I... I thought this might be a short cut... sir.' Malach closed his eyes, waiting for the inevitable cry of alarm or the excruciating pain of death meted out Sable blade.

'Well, you had better get along... and next time don't think!'

Malach kept is eyes closed, he took a couple of deep breaths as the voice turned and started to walk away down the corridor.

The protector continued through the maze of corridors, he had not come face to face with anymore dark angels although he had heard their voices behind ajar doors. The Fallen city was made up of large pantheons which housed certain areas of their city, be it, residential areas, woodland, labour chambers, all linked by a network of corridors. He now stood in an alcove, just large enough for him to be able to stand tall. At the end of this corridor were two immense elaborately ornate doors. Malach thought this must be the entrance to the great hall. He looked around the corridor which was now more like a high elongated chamber in itself, high in the vaults were the scenes of some past battle carved in the roof. He was sure he could make out some movement within the carvings, the carved images replaying the battle over and over again. He leant back into the alcove, it's shadow hiding him from view.

How can I get past the guards? What is beyond the door even if I did get past them? Malach closed his eyes and tried to gather his thoughts. He had been lucky so far, extremely lucky. He had expected to have met many more obstacles than he had, it was obvious the corridors were simply rabbit runs to the major living and working areas of the city. Malach leant forward again and looked down towards the doors, the guards were still there. Under his breath he laughed, what did you expect, the more you look the greater the chance they may have magically disappeared? The more he urged his mind to come up with a plan which would get him past the guards and through the doorway without being seen, the greater the desperation which enveloped him. Malach felt the alcove close in around him, pressing in tighter and tighter. He pressed his back hard into the wall, the wall was pushing him forward out into the corridor into the full view of the Fallen guards. He became desperate, clamping his mouth tight, urging the cry that wanted to escape to remain inside, hidden.

In the distance, from where he had come he could hear footsteps echoing down through the passageway. The alcove sprang back into it's original form as his senses honed into the noise coming closer. Malach was sure this was a sizeable group, and marching. From his right he could hear the great doors swinging open. The orbs on the wall snapped in protest as the protector felt a rush of air flow past him. Rows of Sable Core began to file past Malach, the emblem of the white dagger through angel wings emblazoned against the deep black of their shields. Malach counted eight rows so far, each row containing three dark angels.

As the last row passed him, he saw the opportunity. He jumped out from the security of the alcove. Placing himself behind the middle soldier in the last row. He skipped attempting to match the steps of the group, as they approached the huge open archway Malach strained to make himself look taller, pulled back his shoulders, pulled the shield closer to him. He couldn't see the two guards on opposite sides of the door but he knew they would be there, he knew he stuck out pitifully. He waited for the end which was surely approaching. Carrying on through the doorway drawn to the core of angels like iron filings to a magnet, he passed the guards at the entrance and waited for the cry that would bring death in an instant.

As he walked under the archway he jumped to the side into the deep shadows, his luck had held out. Malach stood absolutely still, becoming one with the darkness. The Sable Core carried on into the centre of the huge hall then split into three separate columns, one on either side of the chamber, the other along the front of the dais, creating a gap in front of the throne. Malach looked to the far end, he could see another set of great doors, more magnificent than any others he had ever seen., They looked as if they could withstand the might of any force in existence. Malach recognised the image of Azazel carved on one door, the other held an equally impressive image of Semhaza. Six pillars on either side of the hall rose high towards the ceiling vault, similar carvings to the ones in the roof of the passageway, intermingled with creatures, a mixture of dragons and wolves covered the pillars. He placed his shield against the wall, making sure the white emblem faced inwards so it would not reflect back into the hall. He unclipped his helmet and placed it behind the shield, concerned the white plume may give away his presence.

The Sable Core lining the hall snapped to attention as a small door on the other side of the great pantheon opened. Lucifer followed by Dalkiel entered through the door. Malach noticed another large dark angel on the far side of the dais, he came into view as he stepped from behind the large throne. The dark angel wore a heavy fur pelt; the protector had not seen this angel before, he looked a war worn angel, his features were rough, his wings powerful but ragged. Within the square of Sable Core, he saw three other angels, his view partially blocked by one of the pillars.

Lucifer sat on his throne. Zaebos stood on one side. Dalkiel on the other standing a little further back.

'What news Dagon?' Lucifer asked.

Malach saw the taller of the three angels step forward, he bowed and then took a few more steps towards the dais.

'My prince the siege goes as planned. We have probed their forces on one occasion with some success. For the most part our stay has been without hindrance.'

'For the most part?' Lucifer questioned.

'The Enlightened foolishly sent a scout into the camp. He was discovered and despatched most appropriately, in a way that sent a very forceful message to all those within the walls of the angel city.'

Malach's mind began to spin, the realisation the kingdom was under attack was too much for him to take in.

'Excellent. Do we know what the situation is like within the walls?' Lucifer stopped and glanced around the hall, he could sense something but was unsure what. Malach froze.

Dagon continued. 'Unfortunately my prince the information we have is extremely limited. Thus far we have been unable to make contact with our informant within the city.'

Informant.....what does he mean informant? Malach grasped at the words searching for the meaning.

Lucifer paused in thought. 'It will be necessary to find a way to make contact with the consort. They will have vital information regarding the morale of the city and their subsequent plans...naturally the implications of them being discovered needs no explanation.'

Dagon bowed his head 'I understand perfectly. I will seek an opportunity to make contact. But only if all the risks have been kept to a minimum.'

'Have you enough resources, Dagon?' Zaebos interjected.

'I have four legions of Core, two legions of cavalry and one siege battalion. For the purposes of laying siege to the angel city my resources are plenty sire. When we decide to commit to the full assault, I will call upon extra legions.'

Lucifer stood, he spoke with a determined tone.

'Dagon, at this moment all our plans are going exactly as we planned. I want nothing....nothing to get in the way of our final victory. We have in our possession one of the accursed Aquinas' cases. The parchment held within has led us to the boy, he holds the information to the whereabouts of the other three. The daemon has informed us the images within his vision are becoming clearer all the time. Soon we will hold the location of the other three parts of his work. All the pieces are in place. We are making progress, albeit not as quick as I would wish. But, the reward for our patience will be truly magnificent. Within the prophet's work is the code to the creation of the universe. With this code I will have the ability to undo all that is, then create a new cosmos where man will bow before me. Azazel and Semhaza will have their bonds cast aside, the Aleph will fade into nothingness.'

Lucifer returned to his throne.

'If the Enlightened make a move against you it is imperative they fail in pushing you from their realm. If required you will call for extra legions to support you in your quest!'

Chapter Seventeen

Malach's mind spun in a whirlpool of despair. The great hall blurred away into the distance as he grappled with the telling of events that seemed unimaginable. The angel kingdom under siege, their resolve weakened by the presence of an informant within the walls, was this the daemon the dark prince mentioned perhaps. No thought Malach Lucifer mentioned a consort! He edged himself along the wall keeping tight to the shadows which hid his presence, he knew at any moment his escape may be discovered. He had come further than he had thought possible, now with all his being he craved the freedom that existed through the conduit. From the information he had gleaned he knew the conduit was not far beyond the great doors.

One of the great doors had been left ajar. Azazel, sword in hand, shield driving through the twisted bodies of Enlightened soldiers looked down seeking out Malach wherever he went. Malach could see Lucifer continuing his council at the far end of the hall. Malach searched for a way out, there would be guards outside of the hall. He could not see them from where he was, but he knew they would be in position. The protector cussed himself as he remembered he had left his shield and helmet leaning against the wall. He could not see them from where he was, but he could see the shadowy figure of Dalkiel skulking around behind the throne. Malach searched desperately for a way through the great doors and on to the conduit beyond. His panic increasing with every passing moment. Above him a faint ray of light came from a small square window, a large banner hung down the wall beside the great door. He looked back down the hall to see Dalkiel continued to pace, if he stumbled across the discarded shield and helmet he would immediately raise the alarm.

Malach pulled on the banner, it seemed secure. Just to make sure he lifted his feet off of the ground, the banner groaned as it became taut. He would have to take a chance on the banner holding, to fly to the window may create too much commotion.

The banner held firm. Malach grabbed the window sill and pulled himself up through the small opening, the haunches of his wings just managed to squeeze through the opening. He was now standing on a long balcony, three becketed orbs flickered. At the opposite end was a wall. The balcony appeared to have no entrance or means of access. A dead end. Malach wondered whether the wall held a door similar to his cell. On the opposite side of the passageway he could see a similar balcony, leaning tentatively forward he saw two guards standing below him in the corners of the passageway next to the great doors. He looked to his left, the passageway disappeared into the distance; it was similar in size to the one he had come through to enter the great hall. Malach could see another corridor branch off opposite him, a strange blue swirling light emanated from it.

He walked gently along the balcony, the guards could not see him, but they would hear him. A strange hum grew louder as he approached the corridor. Malach crouched as he drew opposite and peered down towards an intoxicating haze of blue.

'The conduit!' Malach gasped.

There was one guard standing next to the conduit, the protector searched for a plan to get him through it.

Come on think! As soon as I drop down from this balcony the guards will see me. The conduit, if it works in the same way as the one to the angel kingdom…..Malach paused. Yes, two angels can pass through the conduit and turn up in completely different areas of the entities world. If I can just get through the door the chances of them following me through…yes!

Malach took a couple of deep breathes, then with a powerful thrust upwards his wings pushed him over the balcony, the protector beat his wings powerfully, the smoky air hanging high in the arched roof of the passageway eddied in dancing circles as he urged himself into a steep dive pulling his wings tight into his body. The guard standing next to the conduit did not see Malach until it was too late to react, the gloom covered the protector's thrust for freedom, a cry surged from deep inside him. A defiant roar.

He felt the cool air against his face, the rush of the spring winds through his wings. Below was the silvery pool of Crawford Lake, the reflection of a night cloud drifted across the surface. He turned sharply and headed for the cover of the wood.

Crouching within the deep undergrowth the sounds of the night surrounded him. He sensed he had been away from the entities' world for some time. At this point he could not tell for exactly how long but Malach felt an air of discontent filter through the night, it was a feeling of deep turmoil within the world, a thick covering of foreboding that confused the protector. Malach stood, the animals who roamed during the hours of darkness took no notice of him, entwined in their own battles of survival of the hunter and the hunted. A dual role which Malach now held. He hunted the daemon that accompanied his entity, he hunted the reasons for the turmoil which held the angel kingdom in the grip of siege, yet he knew he was to be hunted by a foe who would show no mercy.

Cameron pulled the duvet up tight around his neck, leaving only his head exposed to the night chill. The spring sun, whilst growing in strength, was not hot enough to carry the heat of the day into the night. He watched Jetrel slowly step through the beds that held his sleeping friends, they turned and fidgeted as he passed. His conversation with the angel at the knoll replayed over and over in his mind. Cameron was not entirely comfortable with it's presence; he could not explain why, just a feeling. The kind of feelings his mother would say were intuition and should be listened too. Rebecca would spend a great deal of time talking to him and answering all his questions, never did she just say 'because that is how it is', everything had a meaning.

Cameron could hear Jetrel somewhere in the corner of the large dormitory, if everything had a meaning, why was I able to see Malach? Why did no one else see their angel or any angel for that matter? Cameron was confused, he could not grasp any of the 'meanings' behind what he was going through, or seeing. This in itself made him feel very uncomfortable. This emotion would cause Jetrel problems seeing through Cameron's thoughts, and ultimately into the vision. An angel required his entity to be completely open to belief, the slightest chink would present a barrier through into their mind and the world beyond. Cameron's eyes became heavy, he closed them and drifted off into a deep sleep. Tomorrow he would go home for the weekend, before flying to Rome on Monday.

The morning sun broke through into the dormitory, Cameron was already awake. Rome, he had heard his father talk about it, describing the mixture of the old city with the sprawling iconic modern day city. He had spoken to Josh last night about fighting just like the gladiators in the arena of the Colosseum. Although Cameron's Colosseum would be a modern gymnasium.

Although Cameron had packed his bag before he went to bed, he attentively picked through each item, making sure he had not forgotten anything.

'Your up early, couldn't sleep?' Josh sat up on his elbows, his hair a tangled mop. He blinked in the sharp sunlight coming through the dormitories large windows.

'No' replied Cameron with a laugh.

'You all set?' Josh said through a yawn.

'Pretty much. Restricted in what we can take because of the weight and stuff, but I have got all the essentials including my camera. I'm sure Emily will look in despair at my attempt at packing a case though.' Cameron leant on the lid of his small case and grunted as the contents resisted, he pulled the zip in short bursts, easing small sections of the zipper together as he did so.

Josh laughed, 'if you have forgotten anything Cam it looks as if it is too late to add it.'

Cameron sat on his bed opposite Josh who had now

pulled himself out of his bed, stretching his arms in a long drawn out groan. 'I wish you were able to come Josh,' Cameron said gently.

Josh smiled, he could hear the hurt in his friends voice. Only Josh could have sensed the true meaning behind the veiled words, he knew Cameron would have given anything for his mother to have been in Rome with him. He was an extremely poor substitute, thought Josh, but he understood the need for Cameron to have the reassurance of familiarity in a strange place. Josh was always struck by the way Cameron could look at one moment, fragile, then confident and bold, an unbeatable force that commanded the arena with the lunge and flick of his rapier.

'I wish I was coming too Cam. We could have marched through the triumphal arch like two Praetorian guards. Then gone on to the senate and saved Caesar from a savage uprising of invading barbarian hordes,' Josh chuckled.

Cameron smiled at the thought of his rotund friend as a hero of imperial Rome.

'It would be me holding back the hordes Josh, and you supervising whilst enjoying suckling pig,' jibed Cameron.

Josh nodded displaying a satisfied grin.

'Well on that note it must be time for a bit of brekkie then?' Josh slapped his stomach and rubbed his hand in a vigorous circle.

Malach hovered outside the window, he could see the two blurry images of Josh and Cameron talking. It had been the first time he had seen his entity, for what to him seemed like an eternity. He was careful not to probe into the inner mind of Cameron too far, his presence would be easier to detect by the daemon if he attempted to unlock the barrier in Cameron's mind. Cameron's excitement allowed the images and thoughts of the fencing competition, and his trip to Italy to press forward beyond his personal barrier.

The protector knew he should return back to the cover of the woods, he wanted to stay with Cameron, to enter the dormitory, but he knew that to clash with the daemon, having escaped the clutches of the dark would be extremely foolhardy. The Fallen would sooner or later seek his presence around Cameron. Malach spread his wings, with a slow pulse he hovered, reluctant to leave Cameron once again, through the dormitory window he could see the two boys were no longer at their beds. He paused for just a moment longer before returning to the wood.

He sat against the trunk of a large oak tree, which grew in the very centre of the wood. It had witnessed the changing landscape over three hundred years. As a sapling it grew within a forest of oak, the forest was felled during the 18th and 19th centuries and used within the battle ships that held the great armies of Europe at bay. It was the sole survivor of an age which turned the landscape from a carpet of ancient canopies into rolling plains of green countryside. Malach's oak tree had seen the reign of twelve monarchs, industrial and modern day technical revolution, the building of an empire, then it's fall; and the estate of a rich Victorian business man was now a school. The oak tree was now a solitary king amongst the Elm and Birch trees.

The warm rays of the sun probed through the leafy roof, around him he saw the plants twist and turn seeking out the rare heat breaking through to the floor. I can't approach Cameron as I am, the daemon will attack even if he is not aware of my escape, which he is sure to be by now. I cannot risk trying to get through the conduit to the city. Cameron is my most pressing responsibility at the moment, my news will have to wait…..Malach toyed with the realisation that any delay in contacting the angel city regarding the news about an informant, may very well be putting the very kingdom itself in peril. If I am caught again then all is lost anyway, I will seek the will of the entity…..then find a way back into the kingdom!

Malach prepared himself for the next stage, he could not approach Cameron within any workable distance, the daemon would sense his presence. He could use the form of an entity, but this was only a smoke screen that worked on man. The protector would need to go further, a decision not taken lightly by any angel. He would take on the soul of an entity.

A sudden gust of wind blew through the tree tops as if the councils of the Aleph were sending a message of caution. Malach knew he was going to be taking a big risk. He would retain only but a few of his angelic powers, but importantly his angelic presence would be beyond the sight of The Fallen.

Malach stood, closed his eyes and paused before taking a deep breath.

'I call upon the watchers of souls…..release me from the shackles of my spirit….I claim the gift of bearing the soul of man…..'

Malach's voice cried out as the winds strengthened, the clouds began to sail across the sky.

'Be it not for the good of my own chalice…..but that of my entity…..grant me the key to reverence…..to serve!'

A sharp light paralysed Malach, his arms raised to the sky, he cried out. His wings shrank into his body, he shook with greater violence as his wings slowly disappeared. His eyes turned to a dark brown becoming the windows into his newly acquired soul. The protector fell to his knees. Exhausted, he dug his hands into the earth stopping himself collapsing completely. He pulled one of his hands up sharply as the shell of an acorn dug into the fat muscle of his thumb, the pain startled him. The realisation of what he had done overwhelmed him.

Sebastian smiled warmly as he heard Cameron running up and down the stairs. Raiding the kitchen while Emily was out he guessed. He had missed him. His work regarding the brutal murders of Pope Steven and the Archbishop of Canterbury had become a massive toll on his time. Before he realised days had passed, then a phone call from Cameron or a message through Emily, would make him angry with himself. He had always been a career man, but following Rebecca's death, he had vowed he would not allow his attention to sway away from what was really important in his life, his family, Cameron. He gathered up the paperwork which was spread across his desk and piled it in a messy heap on top of the cabinet behind his chair. Hanging off of the far corner of his table sat two pieces of paper given to him by Cameron before dashing out of the study. The top paper was Cameron's confirmation sent by the Great Britain Fencing Association, underneath was a paper containing some writing that Sebastian recognised as his son's writing.

Job Chapter 7:13 'Then thou scarest me with dreams, and terrifiest me through visions.'
    Words by Enoch have been ordered hidden by religious theologians and leaders of man's faith. Each are at best

fools, at worse soldiers of The Fallen. My life's work has been to bring forth the light on the hidden message within his words. For these words hold a cataclysmic path towards darkness. The two originators of doubt, greed and deceit, Azazel and Semhaza will cast away their fiery chains of bondage and reap upon this world the flames of destruction. Then the new creation of their world will putrefy in man's reverence towards the great dark angel.

Luke Chapter 21:33 'Heaven and earth shall pass away; but my words shall not pass away'

Within these words is the key to the creation of all that is and all that will be. With the key the powers of darkness will be able to undo the fibres of this world. The world of Adam will be built upon the desires of the Prince of The Fallen. Lucifer will reign over a universe of perpetual darkness, far removed from the light we now know. The words of Enoch will be sent to the four corners of the earth. For his scriptures must remain within the body of the earth, a testament to our being. The key has been removed from the text and destroyed, along with Enoch's original work. The key has passed through the heat of fire into the consciousness of my being, disappearing with the passing of my last breath, only to be seen again with the last of my bloodline.

Sebastian sighed, the one aspect of Cameron's schooling he tried to avoid if at all possible was his homework. He hoped this was not the product of years of expensive English lessons. Sebastian upon scanning the paper again, was drawn to the phrase 'soldiers of The Fallen'. He put his reading glasses down with the piece of paper.

He rubbed his chin, scratching the stubble and turned

towards the door of the study which was slightly ajar. His mind searching out his son, why would Cam have a piece of writing containing a mention of The Fallen. He thought. What kind of work is he doing at school?

The coach pulled up outside the airport terminal. Cameron peered outside of the window at the throng of people arriving and departing through the large doorway, jostling each other as they went about their journeys. He jumped as a piercing shrill suddenly blasted from the coach speakers.

'Can I have your attention!' requested the courier. 'Now then, listen to me carefully. We are going to enter the terminal where you will be met by your team captains. We have plenty of time before the flight leaves, so we are going to split you into your teams, and get everything, as best as we can, organised now. This will save us a lot of time when we arrive in Rome and hopefully will allow us to get to the hotel, grab something to eat and have some time to go for a wander around the city centre......' another sharp whistle reverberated around the coach, '...sorry about that. So, as I was saying, we are going into the terminal. Do not worry about your luggage all that is going to be sorted for you. When you get into the terminal do not wander off! It is important that you stay together....understood?'

The boys acknowledged the courier and as one twisted mass tried to pile out of the coach at the same time. Upon entering the terminal they were spilt into their age groups by the team captains. Cameron knew all the boys in his team, he had fought against all of them at some time during the county and national competitions. He sat quietly alone with his thoughts as all the preparations were being carried out. The bustling noise of the airport terminal going unnoticed as he thought of his mother, the last time he had travelled on a plane it was going on a holiday with her and his father. Shortly after, she was killed in the car accident. Cameron looked forward to seeing his father, but the same old grip of pain that welled up from deep inside began to flow throughout his body, tightening his throat as he suppressed it's release. He quietly moved his thoughts onto his dreams. He did not get the opportunity to discuss the translation he and Josh had worked on with his father. The dream intrigued him more and more, a distraction from the continuous presence of his loss, he mulled over the meaning behind the vision. The purpose of the old man's work.

'Hello Cameron.'

Cameron looked up to see the courier standing over him. A warm smile greeted him through a neat stubbly growth of facial hair. The courier's broad shoulders blocked out the high fluorescent lights of the airport.

'Hello' replied Cameron with a hard swallow.

'May I?' the courier gestured to the empty chair next to him.

'Erm....yes'

'Excited?'

'Yes' Cameron said unconvincingly, his hurt betrayed the fact he was indeed very excited.

'But?'

'Sorry?' replied Cameron.

'I detect a hint of sadness?'

Cameron took another long, hard swallow. Composing himself, he pushed himself back in the chair pressing his back into the rest so he sat up straight.

'No I'm ok. A little tired, I didn't sleep very well last night.'

The courier smiled.

'That's understandable.' The courier paused, and stared at the mass of people, busy with their individual lives, their individual dreams, their individual fears. 'You have a tough fight ahead Cameron.'

Cameron frowned at the courier who met his stare, looking deep into his eyes. 'I am not afraid of anyone, I can....'

The courier laughed softly. 'I hear you are extremely talented with the Rapier. It is not that fight I speak of. I think you have an idea of what I am talking about. You are not alone, you are accompanied by those who would use your insight for their own aims. But, you are watched by one who would protect you from those!'

'I don't understand, what are you talking about?' asked Cameron.

The courier stared into the whirlpool of activity within the terminal, then looked at Cameron and gestured to him to look. Cameron bewildered saw everything moving in slow motion. The clock on the wall to his left had seemingly stopped, the second hand now moving in minute intervals. The faintest hint of cinnamon filled his nostrils.

'Events have taken place which are aimed at securing your belief in a path that is as yet still unknown. You have an insight into a realm which confuses you, yet does not vex you. It is the confusion and the lack of understanding which is your weakness. A weakness which is being exploited by powers you could never imagine, yet will have to face.'

The courier's words puzzled him yet he understood.

'Who are you?' Cameron asked.

'Malach. My name is Malach!'

Cameron watched the courier walk away, his mind now bursting with muddled thoughts, new sensations filled his body. He stared after him in bewilderment. Cameron was distracted, out of the corner of his eye he saw a white snowflake fall towards him. He turned to see it was actually a white feather floating from the ceiling. He followed it's see-sawing flight carefully until it settled at his feet. He picked it up and twiddled it in his fingers, the words of the courier Malach, resonating in his mind.